W9-BEC-947

Adventure Awaits

A **BAXTER FAMILY CHILDREN** *Story*

Adventure Awaits

KAREN KINGSBURY

and TYLER RUSSELL

A Paula Wiseman Book

Simon &

NEW YORK •

Fountaindale Public Library District
300 W. Briarcliff Rd.
Bolingbrook, IL 60440

SIMON & SCHUSTER BOOKS FOR YOUNG READERS
An imprint of Simon & Schuster Children's Publishing Division
1230 Avenue of the Americas, New York, New York 10020

Text © 2022 by Karen Kingsbury
Karen Kingsbury is represented by Alive Literary Agency, 7680 Goddard Street, Suite 200, Colorado Springs, CO 80920, www.aliveliterary.com
Illustrations © 2022 by Olivia Chin Mueller
Jacket design by Laurent Linn © 2022 by Simon & Schuster, Inc.

For information about special discounts for bulk purchases, please contact Simon & Schuster Special Sales at 1-866-506-1949 or business@simonandschuster.com.
The Simon & Schuster Speakers Bureau can bring authors to your live event. For more information or to book an event, contact the Simon & Schuster Speakers Bureau at 1-866-248-3049 or visit our website at www.simonspeakers.com.
Interior design by Laurent Linn
The text for this book was set in ArrusBT Std.
The illustrations for this book were rendered digitally.
Manufactured in the United States of America
0122 FFG
First Edition
2 4 6 8 10 9 7 5 3 1
CIP data for this book is available from the Library of Congress.
ISBN 9781665908023
ISBN 9781665908047 (ebook)

To Donald, my love of thirty-three years,
and to my children and grandchildren, life with
you has always been the greatest adventure. From
Austin's baseball games and EJ's soccer matches, to
seeing Kelsey and Tyler in a dozen CYT musicals . . .
through hiking the Arizona mountains and exploring
the Northwest's Columbia Gorge, and now to the
thrill of finding new adventures with our precious
little ones, this life is a gift. I love you always and
forever, and I thank God for you all.
—Karen

To the reader, wherever you are and whatever your
age, may you keep your eyes open to the adventures
that await you. Thank you for reading these stories.
Thank you for your enthusiastic letters, responses,
and support. If no one has told you today, you are
special. To my family, thank you for all the ways you
have blessed my life and for all the adventures we've
had together. Can't wait to see what awaits us in the
chapters ahead. And to my Lord and Savior, Jesus
Christ. All I have and all I do is because of You and
for You. Thank you for giving me stories to share.
I pray I tell them well. Happy reading, friends.
—Tyler

Dear Reader,

Life is full of adventures, but sometimes you have to look for them. In this book, the Baxter family children are wanting an adventure. A cruise maybe, or a trip to someplace beautiful and beachy. When that doesn't happen, they learn an important lesson: You can find adventures in the everyday.

We hope that as you read about the Baxter children's various adventures in this book, you will begin to find even more exciting moments in your own life. God has great plans for you and those plans include finding the fun even on a rainy Monday afternoon. He tells us to be happy and thankful as much as possible!

But first, get ready for what's ahead . . . the adventure of reading this very special book! You never know what will happen with Brooke, Kari, Ashley, Erin, Luke, and their dog, Bo. But turn the page!

Because Adventure Awaits!!

Love, Karen
and Tyler

BROOKE BAXTER—an eighth grader at Bloomington Middle School in Indiana. She is studious and smart and happy about her family's move. Like before, she has her own room.

KARI BAXTER—a sixth grader at Bloomington Elementary School. She is pretty, kind, and ready to make new friends—even if that means starting a new sport. Out in their huge backyard, Kari and Ashley find the perfect meeting spot for the family.

ASHLEY BAXTER—a fifth grader at Bloomington Elementary. When life gets crazy, Ashley is right in the middle of the mess. Always. She is a dreamer and an artist, open to trying new things. She sees art in everything, and is easily the funniest Baxter child.

ERIN BAXTER—a third grader at Bloomington Elementary. She is quiet and soft-spoken, and she loves spending time with their mom. She has her own room in the new house.

LUKE BAXTER—a second grader at Bloomington Elementary. He's good at sports, but sometimes he's a little too risky. Most of all he's happy and hyper. He loves God and his family—especially his sister Ashley.

1

Monday Surprise

ASHLEY

If only there were a pause button on life.

Then Ashley Baxter would still be watching last night's meteor shower over Bloomington instead of sitting here stuck in school. She tapped her fingers on her desk. Ashley liked school, she really did. But the meteor shower was the best thing she'd ever seen. She and her siblings laying on a blanket under the night sky watching one fireball after another blaze across the darkness.

That was a moment she would've stayed in forever.

Monday morning in Mr. Garrett's class was a very different story. It gave Ashley a sluggish feeling. This wasn't their teacher's fault. Mr. Garrett was at the front of the class talking about the Harrier Reef. Something like that.

Mr. Garrett pointed to a few printed photographs taped to the board. "This is a place in Australia that houses hundreds of types of animals and plant life."

What? Ashley sat up a little straighter. Hundreds of different animals and plant life? Now they were getting somewhere. But why was it called harrier? One photo showed a long line of pretty underwater orange rocks with what looked like a million white tiny strings floating up. Ashley squinted and stared at the picture. *That must be the hair,* she told herself. Coming out of something Mr. Garrett called *Coral. That had to be the reef part, probably.*

Ashley nodded to herself. *The Harrier Reef.*

"Australia's Barrier Reef is an incredibly special geographical and scientific phenomenon." Mr. Garrett seemed very excited. "Not just for Australians, but for people all over the world."

Barrier Reef. It was the Great Barrier Reef! *What was a barrier?* Ashley wondered. And why was it so great? Ashley frowned. School was confusing, especially on Mondays.

Ashley rested her forehead on her desk. Focus was a very difficult thing for her today.

Mr. Garrett kept talking on and on and on. His voice sounded like *WompWompWompBlapBleepBloop*. Ashley placed her hands over her ears. This must be how Charlie Brown felt when his teacher talked. All sound, no words. Ashley closed her eyes. Then her teacher's voice grew quiet. And behind Ashley's closed eyeballs, she began to see stars shooting through the darkness.

She blinked her eyes open, and the bright lights stopped. Once again Ashley closed them, and the shooting stars happened once more. She was on to something here. Open eyes, no shooting stars. Closed eyes, a million of them.

Almost like she had her own superpower.

Ashley felt herself drift up, up into the sky with the meteors. They darted and flew past her, but they were friendly, somehow. And they called to her. "Come, Ashley. Take a ride with us!"

And so, she grabbed hold of the next meteor that passed by and whizzz! She was on a journey, racing through the dark sky, the cool wind in her face.

"Hold on!" the meteor called out to her. And they were flying even faster across space. And suddenly from up ahead—

"Ashley!" The voice did not belong to the meteor—

Someone was tapping on her arm.

With each tap, more of the nice meteors disappeared from the sky. The night wind stopped, too. Ashley opened one eyelid. "What . . . ?" She opened the other one. "Where are the meteors?"

"Ashley . . . this is school." Mr. Garrett was standing beside her. "You cannot sleep on your desk."

Suddenly Ashley sat straight up. A quick look around the room and she could see the unfortunate truth. Her classmates were all watching her. She cleared her throat. "That, my friends, is called a power nap." She nodded to them and then to Mr. Garrett. "You should try it."

Mr. Garrett did not smile or laugh, the way her friends did. "It is time to learn, Ashley. This is not the place for any sort of nap."

"Yes." Ashley nodded. "I'm sorry." She paused. "Long weekend."

Mr. Garrett removed his glasses and pinched the bridge of his nose. "Just try to stay awake, okay?" He walked back to the front of the classroom and continued.

Ashley gave a wink at Elliot, the boy sitting beside her. "Power naps are the best," she whispered.

Elliot's eyes darted to their teacher and back to Ashley. He shook his head real fast. Like he was trying to help Ashley avoid saying anything else. Elliot was one of Ashley's unlikely and very fun friends. The kid was smart and creative and serious about school. Even on a Monday, apparently.

"Moving on," Mr. Garrett gave them a weak smile. "Next, I have big news, class." He walked to his desk and took a stack of packets. He began passing them out.

Elliot leaned closer to Ashley. "I thought learning about the Great Barrier Reef was going to be boring." He took his glasses off and cleaned them with his shirt. "Wow, was I wrong! Pinch yourself to stay awake, Ashley. This stuff is gold." Elliot slammed his glasses back into place and smiled.

Ashley released a tired breath. Maybe if they

actually went to Australia. That would be interesting. She yawned and remembered Elliot's advice. *Fine,* she told herself. Then, with Elliot watching her, Ashley pinched the skin above her elbow. Hard. A yelp slipped through her mouth.

"Not so hard!" Elliot whispered. "You really are one of a kind, Ashley Baxter."

"True." Ashley shrugged. The pinch still hurt, but Elliot was right—Ashley did feel more awake. She tucked this trick away for future Mondays.

Sitting on the other side of Ashley was her friend Natalie. Like always, Natalie looked perfectly put together. Right down to her bright white sneakers and the pink laces. Natalie's hands were folded on her desk, her eyes on Mr. Garrett. Natalie never fell asleep at school. She got all A's and turned her work in neat and on time.

But even with all that, Natalie was a great friend. Elliot and Natalie were proof that friends didn't have to be the same as you.

Mr. Garrett handed Ashley several stapled pages and then he returned to the front of the classroom. "We have a very exciting trip coming up." He began writing on the board.

Ashley read along as he wrote. *Science camp.* Ashley sat up a bit straighter. Okay, now *this* was interesting.

"Science camp is in eleven days." Mr. Garrett smiled at the students. "The packets I gave you explain the details. You will take those home today and get them signed." He paused. "This is an annual trip for fifth and sixth graders. It is an honor. A rite of passage of sorts."

"Rite of passage?" Chris asked out loud from the back of the room. He sounded confused. Chris used to be a menace. But he'd been nicer to Ashley lately, ever since she beat him in a footrace.

Ashley turned around to look at Chris, and that's when she spotted Landon Blake. Landon was her friend, too. He smiled at her and nodded, which was Landon's way of saying hello without words. Landon was good at sports. He was also smart and brave, like the time he helped a group of them escape a crazy corn maze.

Landon was one of the good ones, that's what Ashley's dad said.

Mr. Garrett walked halfway to Chris. "A rite of passage is an event marking an important time in someone's life." Their teacher sounded happy about this. "Every fifth and sixth grader before you has gone to science camp. It's part of growing up in the Bloomington School District."

Ashley thought about that. Science camp. Was it far away? Or possibly like church camp? Back in Michigan, where Ashley and her family were from, church camp happened in the summer. They sang songs and did crafts and played fun games. Maybe science camp was like that.

"Now. Some of you may wonder what science camp is." Mr. Garrett's eyes practically danced with excitement. "It's something like church camp, if you've ever been to one of those."

Ashley slunk down a little in her seat. What was this? Mr. Garrett could read her mind. That was apparently his superpower.

"Science camp lasts a few days and is far away in the woods," Mr. Garrett explained. "We will take a bus there, and we will stay in cabins at night. In the daytime, we will explore nature and do experiments." He was back at the front of the classroom again.

All at once the boys and girls started to talk. Natalie grabbed Ashley's arm. "Hey, let's be in the same cabin!"

From the back of the room, Chris shouted, "I want to see a volcano!"

Yes, Ashley thought. She wanted that, too! Wherever this faraway science camp place was, surely there would be a real-life volcano!

Mr. Garrett raised his hand, and the students stopped talking. "Science camp is very exciting. I'll explain more later." He held up one of the packets. "For now, remember to get this signed by your parents or guardians. It is expected that every student attend. Please return your packet with an adult's signature by Wednesday."

The lunch bell rang.

"All right." Mr. Garrett walked to the door and propped it open. "Let's line up."

The students grabbed their lunch bags and coats and fell into single file.

A million questions flooded Ashley's mind.

Science camp sounded like an incredible adventure. She couldn't wait to talk about this with Elliot and Natalie.

Once they were seated at their lunch table, science camp came up right away.

"Science camp is my biggest dream." Elliot dunked a carrot in ranch dressing and chomped on it. "I've been to a different science camp before. With my family."

"What's it like?" Natalie sounded a little nervous. She pulled a peanut butter sandwich from her lunch bag. "It could be scary, you know."

Ashley patted her friend's arm. "Don't be afraid, Natalie. God is with you. That's what my mom and dad always say." Ashley leaned closer to her friend. "It's in the Bible."

"Okay." Natalie seemed to relax. "I'll try to remember that."

Elliot raised both hands high over his head, which made his glasses fall a few inches down his nose. He fixed them and lifted his hands again. "Science camp is the best time. You collect samples and study different species and walk through streams."

He seemed to run out of air. He took a drink of water and continued. "At least that's what we did."

"What about experiments?" Ashley finished the last of her fruit snacks. "Scientists always do wild, amazing experiments. Like with green gloop or electricity."

Natalie furrowed her brow. "I think that stuff is only in movies."

"Actually"—Elliot spoke up—"Ashley is right. But I don't think fifth and sixth graders are allowed to do those experiments. That's for adults."

Ashley crossed her arms. "I'm not sure I want to go if there are no gloopy experiments. What else is there?"

"Ashley, I know you. You'll love it. I promise." Elliot slipped his lunchbox into his backpack and gasped. "Oh! I almost forgot." He pulled out two envelopes and handed one to Ashley and the other to Natalie.

"A Monday gift!" Ashley squealed. "I love Monday gifts."

Natalie stared at her. "What exactly is a Monday gift?"

"It's this!" Ashley tore open the envelope. "A gift on a Monday just cause it's Monday, right, Elliot?"

He blinked. "Um . . . actually—"

Before he could finish, Ashley pulled a metallic piece of cardboard from the envelope.

"It's an invitation." Elliot gave Ashley a high five. "To my Super-Duper Birthday Bonanza. This Saturday." He hesitated, very dramatic. "And guess what? The whole class is invited. And I'm having team challenges. And junk food. Plus, you can wear a costume!"

"Wow!" Ashley stared at the invitation. "I've never even heard of a Super-Duper Birthday Banana, Elliot." She thought for a minute. "Are we supposed to bring bananas? Or are we making fried bananas? Maybe I could dress up as a banana."

Elliot blinked a few times. Like he wasn't sure what to say.

Natalie giggled. "*Bonanza*. Not banana, Ashley." Natalie looked at Elliot. "Ashley gets words mixed up sometimes."

"True." Elliot smiled in Ashley's direction. "When that happens, Ashley, I'll help you, my friend."

"Me, too," Natalie nodded. "You need a lot of help, Ashley."

Ashley did a bow. "That's all I need. A lot of help from my friends." She pressed the shiny paper to her heart. "*Bonanza!* Wow!" Her mind was spinning with excitement. "What does it mean?"

"It means fun!" Elliot looked proud of himself. "An adventure day of fun. And the whole class is invited."

"Really?" Ashley jumped in a few small circles, waving the invitation in front of her. "I've always wanted to go to an adventure party." Her voice sounded dreamy. "Thank you, Elliot. Your birthday bonanza will definitely be one of the highlights of my life."

"It will." Elliot pumped his fists in the air. "That's why it's a bonanza."

Ashley stuck the invitation in her lunchbox. "Also, I can't wait to meet your parents. Because I bet they're interesting, like you."

"About that." Elliot frowned, like he had sudden bad news. "Ashley . . . my parents, they're suspicious about you."

"What?" Ashley's eyes grew wide. "Why me?"

"They heard about the corn maze." Elliot made a concerned face. "And about you getting us in trouble for that group drawing last week when Mr. Garrett was teaching. And they saw you go sort of do your own thing at the talent show . . . and that time when—"

"Okay, okay." Ashley crossed her arms. "You have a point. But those are just a few moments. That's not who I am." She found her smile again. "I'll change their mind at the party. You'll see. Then they won't be suspicious. They will be . . . happy-icious." Ashley nodded. Yes. She would show them just how amazing and trustworthy she was.

After lunch was library time. Ashley had just finished *Charlotte's Web*. It was an intense story about barnyard animals and a talking pig, and a spider who risks her life to save the day by writing messages in her web. But really the story was about friendship. And courage.

The spider reminded her of Landon Blake.

After she slipped *Charlotte's Web* onto the return

cart, Ashley walked over to the desk of Ms. Forrest, the librarian.

"Ms. Forrest?" Ashley rocked back and forth on her heels.

"Yes, baby?" Ms. Forrest wore colorful flowy outfits. She had beautiful dark curly hair and her eyeglasses hung around her neck like a decoration. "What did you think about *Charlotte's Web*?"

"I liked it. Wilbur was so cute." Ashley smiled. "But the spider was the best."

Ms. Forrest grinned. "I thought so, too. I love Charlotte." She paused. "You looking for another story like it? Or something new?" Ms. Forrest loved helping the students find the perfect book.

"Something new." Ashley tapped her chin. "Maybe a book about science. We're going to science camp, and I have a *lot* to learn."

"Well, what do you know?" Ms. Forrest grinned. "It's science camp time already. You're going to have a blast." She stood. "I have the perfect book for you. Follow me."

The two walked toward the back to a section

called Science. Fitting, Ashley thought.

Ms. Forrest scanned the shelves. "A-ha! Here it is." She pulled out a book and handed it to Ashley. It was a hardback book. "*Scientists that Shaped Society.*" Ms. Forrest sounded proud of herself. "This is just what you're looking for."

Photos of old people decorated the cover. Scientists, Ashley guessed. She blinked a few times. "I was thinking maybe something about volcanoes. I'm really hoping to see one at science camp."

"That's funny." Ms. Forrest laughed. "Give this book a try. I really think you'll like it."

Ashley thanked the woman and headed for the readers' corner. It was a spot in the library with chairs, bean bags, and cozy lighting. In some ways, it was the perfect nap spot. Ashley sat in the nearest bean bag chair. Then she pinched her own arm again.

Just to be sure she didn't fall asleep.

A book about scientists. Ashley studied the cover, then she began to read. In Chapter One, Ashley learned about Marie Curie, a scientist who helped find treatments for cancer. Next was a man named George Washington Carver, famous for his work with soil and crops. He was also an inventor.

Reading hour was almost over, so Ashley closed the book. The librarian had been right. Ashley couldn't wait to read more. Maybe one day she'd be a scientist in a book like this and some fifth-grade kid would read about *her*.

In the time that remained, Ashley sketched herself as the most amazing, world-changing scientist, dressed in a white coat surrounded by coils and test tubes and mixing bowls. The possibilities were endless.

The sketch made Ashley even more excited for science camp. She couldn't wait. Plus, she might just see a real live volcano.

What could be better than that?

2

Back from the Caribbean

KARI

Kari Baxter closed her eyes and listened. The laughter and conversation around her family's kitchen table was the best sound in all the world. Every day after school, Kari looked forward to this, and now that they were all home, she couldn't stop smiling.

Today Mom had made them cheese and crackers and apple slices. The plate sat at the middle of the table while the kids did homework and talked about their day.

In the Baxter family, every day was full of interesting conversations and new surprises. Whether it was a story from her older sister, Brooke; funny moments from their younger sisters, Ashley and

Erin, or some interesting thing from her brother, Luke. Life in this family was the best.

Sometimes Kari liked to just sit back and take it all in.

This was one of those afternoons. Ashley had just finished telling them about science camp. She and her class were taking a bus to some far off place to study nature. Kari was glad science camp was happening to Ashley. Because it was the last place Kari would want to go.

Now Luke was telling a story about his freshly scraped knee from his race with a kid at school. "I would have won if my shoelace was tied." Luke chomped on an apple slice. He was the only boy in the lineup of Baxter kids, and he had just recovered from a broken arm. Now he had a damaged knee.

His injuries were starting to become a trend.

A big bandage covered most of Luke's knee.

"You should take it easy, Luke." Kari patted his shoulder. "There's only so much your body can take."

"True." Luke gave a light touch to his bandaged knee and made a face. "I have a lot of battle scars."

19

As if he could understand what they were talking about, Bo, their new adopted dog, crossed the room and sat at Luke's feet. Luke patted Bo's head. "I coulda beat him, Bo. I'm faster. I know I am."

Bo yawned and laid down on his belly.

"You should be more careful." Erin stared at Luke's knee. "At least tie your shoes." Erin cared about everyone. Kari liked that about their youngest sister.

Ashley seemed to be in her own world. She stared at what looked like a spelling list. "Odd ages." She tapped her pencil on the table. Then she began to spell. "A-U-D-A-C-I-O-U-S."

Brooke looked up from her notebook. "How did you say it?" Brooke was in middle school. She was smarter than all of them put together.

"Odd ages." Ashley shrugged. "It's spelled A-U-D-A-C-I-O-U-S."

"That's *audacious*." Brooke's tone remained kind. "Not odd ages."

"Audacious, hmm. "Ashley lowered her forehead to the table. "What does that even mean?"

Kari giggled. Ashley always made her laugh.

Brooke knew the answer right away. "It means extremely bold. Or daring."

"That's right." Mom spoke up from the kitchen. She was rummaging through the cupboards looking for a fresh bandage for Luke. "It can also mean fearless."

"Hey." Ashley sat back up. "That's like me. Fearless. And bold."

"True." Mom laughed from the kitchen.

Mom walked up with a Band-Aid and some peroxide for Luke. Mom always had an extra Band-Aid. Or a long hug or the time to listen. Every good trait that Kari thought a person should have. Their mom looked at Luke. "Take off the old bandage."

Luke put his leg up on the chair and peeled back the colorful bandage he had gotten at school. "I need to practice tying my shoes."

"Okay. Well, then we will do just that." Mom poured the peroxide on a cotton ball. "Here we go. Take a big breath."

Luke filled his cheeks.

"Ouch. I can't watch." Erin covered her eyes.

"Lemme see." Brooke leaned in. "Look how it

bubbles." Their dad was a doctor, and Brooke had always been interested in medical problems.

Impressive, Kari thought. She, herself, had no interest in being a doctor.

Mom dabbed at Luke's injured knee. "The bubbles mean the peroxide is killing the bacteria. It's working." Mom looked up at Luke. "You okay?"

"Yeah. It . . . doesn't hurt . . . that bad." He was breathing funny. It looked like it hurt a lot.

"You're brave." Kari smiled at their brother. "Way braver than me."

"Thanks." Luke blew out a big puff of air.

Mom covered the scrape with the Band-Aid, kissed her fingers and placed them gently on Luke's knee. "There." She stood. "Better?"

"Better." Luke breathed normal again. "Thanks, Mom."

Kari sandwiched her last piece of cheese between two crackers. She loved this snack.

Suddenly, the doorbell rang.

"That's the Howards." Mom headed for the door. "They're going to tell us about their big cruise! They just got back!"

The Howards lived down the street. They were the first neighbors the Baxters had met when they moved to Bloomington earlier this fall. The Howards had three kids: Steven, Carly and Marsha.

All five kids cleaned the table and put their dishes in the sink. Kari couldn't wait to hear the details. Imagine . . . cruising through the Caribbean.

"Do you think they found treasure?" Ashley dried her hands on the kitchen towel.

Kari shut off the water and took the towel from her sister. "Where would they find treasure?"

"The Caribbean has tons of gold and rubies and diamonds." Ashley looked at her. "I read about it in a book."

"What book?" Kari squinted.

Ashley shrugged. "Some book."

Kari and Ashley joined the others in the living room.

Ashley sighed before she sat down. "I expected to see a chest of some kind," she whispered to Kari. "I'm guessing no treasure."

"Kids, look." Mom held out a striped paper

23

bag. "Mrs. Howard brought us candy from the Bahamas!"

"Cool." Luke jumped up and down. "Thank you."

Kari and the others thanked the woman, too.

"You're welcome." Mrs. Howard's cheeks were tan. "The cruise was just the best time. All around us, the water was clear and pale blue. And the food!" She looked at their mother. "Elizabeth, your family should take a cruise. So many beautiful beaches and sunsets. Yes, cruises are the way to go, for sure." Mrs. Howard took a quick breath. "On the first stop we spent a day on Grand Cayman Island, where we took a Jeep across . . ."

Kari hung on every word. And there were a lot of words, for sure. Mrs. Howard couldn't stop talking about the trip.

By the time Mrs. Howard finally stopped, Kari's mother looked a little dazed. "Well yes, Linda, we would love to take a cruise like that. I think we'll definitely do that someday!" Mom laughed. "Maybe in a few years."

"How about Wednesday?" Ashley jumped up. "The ship is probably filling up right this minute,

Mother. We wouldn't want to miss our spot."

"Ashley." Mom's voice had that final sound, like there was no changing her mind. She smiled at Ashley. "We cannot go this week."

Brooke raised her hand. "I'm with Ashley. I'd like to go as soon as possible. Maybe Friday?"

"Okay." Mom pointed to the backyard. "Why don't you kids go outside? Mrs. Howard and I are going to catch up."

Kari, her siblings, and the Howard kids made their way to the backyard. Luke and Steven grabbed the basketball and ran to the hoop at the edge of the Baxters' driveway. The girls sat on the back porch so they could hear more about the Howards' cruise.

"Marsha. I have to know." Ashley crossed her arms. "Did you find actual treasure?"

"Yes! Except . . ." Marsha reached into her pocket and dug out some gold coins. "We didn't *find* treasure. But we bought these in Nassau." Marsha looked proud of herself. "That's in the Bahamas."

Ashley leaned in to see. "I'll bet they're real." She took one of the coins and examined it.

"I don't know for sure." Marsha handed the other gold pieces to Kari and Erin.

Kari handed the coin back to Marsha. "I have a question." Kari tilted her head. "Was the ocean water warm?" She couldn't wait for another beach trip. It had been more than a year since they'd gone.

"Yes, it was so warm." Marsha closed her eyes. Her smile looked like she was on the cruise again. "It might be fall here, but it was summertime there. The water was clear and soft and the prettiest color. And the sun was hot!"

Erin leaned back on her hands. "What about the waves? Were they big?"

"Not too big." Marsha scrambled to her feet and held out her arms like she was surfing. "We rode boogie boards. It was so fun."

"Let's get back to the treasure." Ashley gathered all the coins in her hands and held them out. "I've seen many pictures of treasure. These are definitely real."

A few feet away Kari could hear Brooke and Carly talking. They were the same age and had a lot in common. A while ago they even did a science project together. A volcano experiment!

Brooke stared at her friend. "You're so tan. And your hair is incredible." Carly's hair had little beads braided into it.

"Everyone gets this done in the Bahamas." Carly smiled. "It took an hour."

Kari looked across the yard at Luke. He and Steven were passing the basketball, and Kari could hear them talking about the Howards' cruise, too. "What was your favorite part?" Luke asked. He dribbled the ball and then tossed it to his friend.

Steven wore a shell necklace and his hair looked blond and beachy. "Everything." He held the ball for a minute. "Plus, the cruise ship had a buffet dinner every night, and you could eat whatever you wanted and as much as you wanted!"

"Really? As much as you wanted?" Luke's jaw dropped.

Kari and the girls were all listening to the boys now.

Steven dribbled the ball and passed it to Luke. "Yep. As much as you want."

Luke set the ball down. "Like hot dogs? And ice cream? And pizza?"

"Yes." Steven laughed. "All of that."

Carly chimed in. "Steven didn't even talk about the water park."

"Water park? With slides?" Kari felt her heart beat faster. "On the cruise ship?"

"Right." Carly smiled so big her lips had to hurt. "I couldn't believe it. We could play in it anytime we wanted."

Marsha stood and did a graceful spin. "But I think my favorite was the captain's dinner."

Kari liked the sound of that. "Does the captain come and eat with you?"

"Who's the captain?" Luke ran over and joined them on the porch.

"He's the guy driving the ship." Steven also sat with the group. "But he doesn't eat with every table."

"No." Marsha giggled. "He walks around and says hello. But we all dress up, so it's like a ball. Like something from a fairy tale."

"Ladies in long dresses. Men in suits." Carly

drew a deep breath and let it out slowly. Like she was floating. "I brought a pretty skirt and shiny black shoes." She clasped her hands together. "It was the best."

Kari watched Ashley's expression change.

"Well . . ." Ashley set the gold coins down. She stood and spun a few times. "I wore a flowy pale blue dress at the talent show last week." She folded her hands. "Which you missed. So . . . basically the same thing."

"Oh." Carly smiled. "Okay. Great."

Kari thought she knew how Ashley was feeling. Like maybe they'd heard enough about the Howards' cruise, no matter how wonderful it had been. After all, the Baxters had gone on just one cruise—on Lake Monroe. Fifteen minutes from home.

Carly and Marsha and Steven must have run out of details to share about their trip, because the boys returned to shooting hoops. Carly and Brooke joined them.

Kari pictured herself on a cruise ship. White gloves and a princess gown. Eating five ice cream cones in a row and slipping down water slides. She turned to

Marsha. "Your vacation sounds amazing." Kari took a slow breath. "Like the greatest adventure."

"It was." Marsha still had that dreamy look on her face. "The very best adventure."

After a moment, Ashley stood and cleared her throat. "Just so you know . . . I'm going on an adventure, also." She put her hands on her hips. "The *actual* best kind."

"Oh." Marsha leaned forward. Her eyes seemed brighter, like she was really interested. "Your family is taking a cruise, too?"

Kari rolled her eyes. *Here we go,* she thought.

"No, no." Ashley shook her head. "Nothing that tame." She paused, like she wanted to build the suspense. "I'm going to . . . science camp." Ashley nodded. Satisfied.

"Science camp?" Marsha's enthusiasm dropped off. "That's just part of school."

"School?" Ashley gasped. "Oh, no, no, Marsha. Clearly you have never experienced the joys of an *adventurous* science camp." She acted out the next part. "The great outdoors . . . The real-life volcanoes . . . sleeping near a babbling creek—

under the stars." Ashley grabbed a quick breath. "And—of course—my favorite . . ." She paused. "Making friends with wild bears."

Marsha scrunched her eyebrows. "Bears?"

"Ashley." Kari shook her head. "You won't be making friends with wild bears."

"I think we will." Ashley seemed very confident.

A giggle came from Kari. "And . . . there won't be real volcanoes. Not at science camp."

Ashley shrugged. "We shall see." She smiled at Marsha. "Time will tell. Either way, science camp is coming. And that—my friend—will be the very biggest adventure."

No one said anything for a moment. It was a lot to take in.

"Well . . . it's not a cruise." Carly patted Ashley's hand. "But have fun with that." She gave Ashley a thumbs-up.

Ashley beamed. "I will have fun!" Her tone was not quite rude, but it was close. "Thank you very much."

Mrs. Howard stepped out onto the porch. "Time to go, kids. Say goodbye."

After the Howards left, quiet came over the house. Kari and her siblings sat back at the kitchen table and began their homework. No more happy talk and laughter. It felt like Ms. Nan's class when they had to take a test.

Finally, Brooke set her pencil down and looked at Mom, a few feet away making dinner. "Please, Mom, can we go on a cruise? I really want to go."

"Me too." Luke grabbed his stomach. "All-you-can-eat pizza!"

Erin closed her book and turned to face their mother. "I can't stop thinking about the ship." She clasped her hands. "We might even see a dolphin."

Their youngest sister had a point. Kari slid her chair back. "Mom, maybe you could talk it over with Dad."

"Children." Mom's smile looked tired of the subject. "We will not be taking a cruise anytime soon." She stirred whatever was cooking on the stove. "But . . . I will talk to your father about it."

Brooke, Luke, Erin, and Kari all cheered. Because at least there was a chance.

The whole time, Ashley had never looked up

from her homework. When the cheering grew quiet, she waved one hand in the air like she was swatting at an invisible fly. "No, Mother. No need to talk to Dad." She still didn't look up. "Who needs a cruise? I get to go to science camp." She gave a sympathy look to Erin and Luke. "And one day . . . you will have science camp, too." She winked. "Something to look forward to, my young siblings."

From the kitchen, Kari saw her mother cover her mouth. But they could all hear her laugh, anyway. Ashley had that effect on people.

Before dinner, Kari found her journal and plopped down on the living room sofa. She turned to the next blank page and began to write.

Hi, there. It's me, Kari. The Howards just came back from a cruise. I wish we could do something like that. Also, today, Ashley found out she is going to science camp. I'm glad my class isn't going! It doesn't sound like fun at all. Muddy shoes, bugs buzzing around. Trying to take notes on messy paper. Plus . . . what if there

really are bears out there? Like Ashley
said there would be?

A shiver ran down Kari's arms.

No bears for her. No faraway science camp, either. Kari would be happy to stay right here in Bloomington and take dance classes. That would be plenty enough fun for her.

At least until the Baxter family took that cruise.

3

Noodle Surprise

ASHLEY

Ashley felt very tall as she stirred the twisty noodles. This was big-kid stuff, working with boiling water in a big pot over a dancing fire. Plus, Mom was just a few feet away, so there was nothing to be scared about.

Kid dinner was a new thing for the Baxter family. Tonight was the first one, after an idea that had come from their mother. "My parents always let me help cook," Mom had told them when they came home from school that day. Which was proof that a person did not need a cruise ship to have an adventure.

After a quick vote, the kids decided to make spaghetti.

Cooking the twisty noodles was Ashley's job. Right next to her, Brooke stirred the hamburger meat. And Kari helped Mom with a red sauce. Across the kitchen, Erin tore up washed pieces of lettuce and put them in a wooden bowl, and Luke painted salty butter over two long sections of bread.

Ashley figured it would be the best spaghetti in the whole world. Since the kids made it, of course.

Brooke looked over her shoulder at their mother. "It's been a whole day since the Howards told us about their cruise." She sounded very polite. Polite sometimes helped get what you want. They all knew that. Brooke continued, "So did you talk to Dad yet . . . about the cruise?"

Mom was sprinkling dark green flakes into the red sauce. She set the tiny bottle down on the counter and looked at Brooke. "I'll let you know when I talk to him." Her voice sounded kind. "In the meantime,"—she pointed to the box of candy the Howards had brought over—"let's be thankful for the gifts the Howards brought us."

Ashley could feel the frustration arrows coming from Brooke's face. She kept her eyes on her noodles.

"Science camp," she whispered. "Just saying."

"Okay." Brooke turned to her. "Did it ever occur to you, Ashley, that I'm too old for science camp?" She looked more sad than angry. "So please . . . stop comparing your class's trip to a cruise. It's not helping."

Ashley jabbed the big spoon at the noodles a few times. "Fine."

Conversation about the cruise was clearly not dying down. Kari looked up from the bowl of sauce. "One day we'll take a trip like the Howards' cruise. Right, Mom?"

"Brooke." Their mother's laugh didn't last long. "We do that all the time. Our trip to the beach . . . that day on Lake Monroe—"

"The 5-K walk." Ashley spoke up. She liked agreeing with her mother. It was new for her. Ashley poked her spoon into the air. "Fun times are what we Baxters are known for." She gave Kari a quick grin. "Everyone wishes they were a Baxter."

"True." Brooke nodded. "You have a point."

"Thank you." Ashley stepped back from the stove, the spoon still in her hand, and did a bow.

"Thank you very much, Brooke."

"Look at this garlic bread!" Luke sounded happy with himself.

Ashley glanced behind her and stared at their brother. He waved the butter knife around like a small sword. He grinned big. "Have you ever seen so much butter?"

Ashley stared at the bread. The butter was as thick as a brownie. "Nope." Ashley shook her head. "In my honest opinion, that is more butter than I've ever seen on any piece of bread."

A slight gasp came from Mom. She hurried over and took the knife from Luke. "Wow. Okay." She set the knife down. "Very nice, Son." With her eyes still staring at the bread, she patted Luke on the back. Then very fast she removed globs of the butter from the bread. "There we go. That's better."

Deep in her heart, Ashley thought Luke's version of the garlic bread might truly taste better. She loved butter. But she kept that thought to herself. A skill she was working on.

Ashley stared at her noodles. She had chosen

the twisty kind because long-noodle spaghetti was boring. Dinner only came around once a day . . . so why not make it special? Ashley gave the noodles another few stirs. Now that they were almost cooked, the water had mostly disappeared. Sitting in a big clump, the noodles didn't look that interesting, after all.

"Hmm." She stirred them again. "What you need is a little pizzazz," she whispered to the twisty things.

Brooke glanced at her. "What?"

"Oh, nothing." Ashley grinned. "Just talking to my noodles. Encouraging them, cheering them on. You know."

Again, she studied the twisty little guys. Then without making any big movements and while staying completely silent, Ashley walked a few feet and opened the spice cupboard. There must've been a hundred small glass bottles and little shakers. What would help the boring noodles?

She tapped her forehead a few times and then she spotted the answer. Right in front of her was a bottle of vanilla. And next to it a small glass shaker of cinnamon. That's what the labels said. Also, she had helped Mom bake cookies last week and they had used both those ingredients.

Ashley hummed a little hum as she took the two bottles back to the stove. She twisted the lid off the vanilla and poured a few drops into the noodles. Then she tilted her head to the side. That would never be enough. She poured a few more splashes into the pan and set the bottle next to the stove.

The whole time Brooke was too busy with the meat to notice.

So, Ashley took the cinnamon bottle, unscrewed the top, and began shaking the pretty brown powder all across the twisty noodles. The smell was delicious.

"Ashley!" Brooke shrieked. She must've been very surprised at Ashley's idea, because she dropped the meat spoon on the floor. Brooke stared at her. "What are you doing?"

At that, Mom rushed over. "Ashley, did you put . . . *cinnamon* in the noodles?" There was a ribbon of panic in her voice.

"Yes, Mother. Yes, I did." Ashley stood even taller. "And also . . . some vanilla."

"What?" Mom slid Ashley to the side of the stove and stirred the noodles. They were a delicious brown color now. Mother's eyes looked frazzled. "What would make you do that?"

"Creativity." Ashley nodded. "And your great advice, of course."

"Mine?" Mom turned to her. "When did I say to make noodles this way?"

"We were making cookies the other day." Ashley felt hurt over her mother's tone. Like Ashley had done something wrong. She repeated her mom's words from that day. "You said cinnamon and vanilla make everything taste better." Her eyes found the noodles again. "And, I will say, Mother, these twisty noodles looked like they needed some help."

Mom closed her eyes for a moment and took a few steps away from the stove. Like she was trying to focus her thoughts. Finally, she looked at Ashley. "You're right. I did say that. But that's for desserts. Not pasta."

Ashley scooted back to her post "Oh." There was more pep in Ashley's spoon as she mixed the noodles this time. "Maybe if I pound on them a little more, the cinnamon and vanilla will stir off."

"Never mind." Mom patted Ashley's shoulder. "Tonight's spaghetti will just be . . . interesting." Mom slipped her hands into her oven mitts and removed the simmering noodles from the stove. "Erin?" Mom called out. "How's the salad?"

"Done!" Erin held up the full bowl of lettuce pieces and set it down next to Ashley's twisty delight.

"We haven't had pasta in a long time." Luke finished washing his hands.

Mom grabbed serving spoons. "Yes. Well, this will be like having it for the first time. Cause it's a new Ashley recipe."

"You're welcome." Ashley looked at the pot. "I call it cinna-noodles. Like snicker-doodles." Ashley thought for a moment. She was making this up as she went along. "Without the Snickers or the doodle." She smiled at the room. "It actually doesn't smell that bad."

Kari peered over Ashley's shoulder at the creation. "I think your part of dinner is unique," Kari said. "Which . . . is only fitting."

The front door opened and everyone exchanged excited glances.

"Dad's home!" Erin squealed.

They took off for the front door. Ashley slid along the wood floor in her socks. The feeling of having her dad come back after a long day at work was one of her favorites. She rounded the corner and there he was. His name tag proudly on his coat.

DR. JOHN BAXTER.

Luke hugged one of Dad's legs and their father lifted Erin up onto his hip. Brooke wrapped her arms around his waist, and Kari hugged him from the side. Ashley stood back a bit, waiting her turn. Her siblings were like monkeys climbing a tree. It looked silly and sweet at the same time. Then, Mom joined them. She leaned in and gave Dad a kiss on his cheek. Ashley smiled. Her parents were writing their own personal love story.

Mom helped Dad take off his coat. "How was work?"

"Just okay." Dad's shoulders slumped a little. "Glad to be home." The other kids stepped back.

Finally, Ashley took her spot beside him. "I made cinna-noodles for the kids' spaghetti dinner."

"Hmm." Her dad ran his hand over Ashley's hair. He smiled at her. "I'm sure it'll be great."

When they were all seated around the table, Dad prayed. But his words were a little quieter than usual.

Mom must've noticed because she put her hand over Dad's. "Tough day, honey?"

"Yes." Dad squeezed her hand. "Hospitals can be hopeful places. But sometimes they can be hard."

"Kinda like school." Ashley understood. "I fell asleep in Mr. Garrett's class."

A tired chuckle left Dad's lips. "That happens."

Kari took a big spoon of the sauce and sprinkled it over the brown cinna-noodles. "I never think about that." She looked at their dad. "How parents can have a rough day, too."

"Yeah." Luke looked at their father. "Maybe after dinner we should shoot hoops, Dad. That always helps me."

"Deal." Dad nodded.

"But God is with you . . . just like you tell us." Erin took a quick drink of her milk. "Right, Dad?"

"Always." Dad moved the bowl of twisty noodles close and took a big scoop. "These are the most interesting noodles I've ever eaten, Ashley."

"That's putting it mildly." Brooke giggled.

Bo, their puppy, circled around everyone's legs, something he wasn't supposed to do. However, he was smart enough to avoid Dad's legs. Ashley could hear him under the table. *Sniff, sniff . . . wag, wag.* Finally, he sat down smack on Ashley's right foot. But he was light, so Ashley let him stay.

Maybe Bo would like a cinna-noodle, she thought. But she decided against it. Ashley peeked under the table and frowned. "Shoo. Go, Bo. I don't want you to get in trouble." Ashley's voice was a whisper.

"You know, Ashley." Luke's cheeks were full of macaroni. Like a squirrel's. "These cinna-noodles aren't bad." He shoved another spoonful in his mouth. "They taste like pancakes. Pancakes with tomato sauce."

"Hmm." Ashley nodded. She wasn't sure that

was a compliment. "Mother? Do you agree?"

Mom smiled and wiped the corners of her mouth with her napkin. "It's unique . . . but yes, I like it. You did just the right amount of vanilla and cinnamon."

"Pizzazz, Ash!" Kari made an invisible rainbow in the air over her head. "You did it!"

Ashley made an equally impressive invisible rainbow. "Pizzazz! I think if art doesn't work out, I could be a chef."

"A chef is like an artist with food." Mom looked at Ashley.

"That's true." Ashley liked this picture. Later she would sketch herself in a tall chef's hat, creating unique recipes at fancy restaurants. Her life was all coming together. Maybe she was onto something.

"Ashley's unusual pancake spaghetti is good. It's true." Brooke laughed. "But can we please get back to the Howards' cruise?" She set her fork down. "If we can't set sail on the Caribbean Sea, maybe we could . . . go to a theme park?"

"True!" Erin chimed in. "Or the zoo!"

Luke grabbed a piece of his buttery garlic bread. A few drops of butter dripped onto the table. "What about a basketball game?" He stuck a chunk of the bread in his mouth. "A real professional one!"

"I'm not too worried." Ashley smiled. "I have science camp. Wild bears and volcanoes." She did a humble nod. "I'm sorry you can't all come."

"I think a shopping adventure would be fun." Kari slid her empty plate away from her. "I need new clothes for dance class."

"Well, it seems like everyone has a good idea for an adventure day." Mom sat back in her seat. "I'm taking notes."

"Here." Luke slid a piece of spaghetti meat under the table. "Easy, Bo!" He shouted.

Dad looked under the table. "Luke? What are you doing?"

"Um." Luke was caught. "Bo looked hungry. I'm sorry."

"Son, we're trying to train Bo." Dad stood. "Come on, Bo." Their father walked the dog to the edge of the kitchen and had him lay down. "There you go. Stay. Good boy."

When Dad returned to the table he smiled at the rest of them. "You know, Bloomington is a great place for adventuring. We don't need a fancy cruise to have fun." Dad crossed his arms. "What about an all-day hike around Lake Monroe! Exploring, seeing the sights, lunch by the shore." He grinned at Luke. "Obviously some fishing!" Dad's face lit up. "We could do that this Saturday morning. How about that?"

The family cheered and clapped. It *was* a great idea. Elliot's birthday party wasn't until later on Saturday, so a morning family adventure would be perfect. Also, Dad looked happier. Like he seemed to have forgotten about his rough day.

Ashley helped clear the table and then she set up at the sink to wash the pans. Kari dried them while Brooke put the leftover food into the fridge. Erin washed the counters, and Luke followed after her with a towel.

Kids' dinner had turned out to be a great idea. Plus, it gave Ashley the emotion of pizzazz and a new dinner dish in case she opened her own restaurant one day. Cinna-noodles.

Because everything really was better with a little vanilla and cinnamon.

Ashley hummed "The Star-Spangled Banner" while she worked. They were learning it in Mr. Garrett's class. She was glad her dad had told them that his day was a little rough. Emotions came with life. But God promised to be there through them all. As she neared the bottom of the sink of dirty dishes, Ashley could barely keep from dancing

Because now she had not one, but two adventures ahead. Plus Elliot's birthday party.

And what could be better than that?

49

4

A Bad News Day

KARI

Kari expected Wednesday to be perfect. She had a hiking adventure to look forward to, her dance lessons started soon, and it was sunny after raining all last night.

But even so, this Wednesday had other plans for her.

The trouble started with Ms. Nan's math lesson. Today they were learning how to add fractions, and all Kari could think about was why? Why learn how to add fractions? How would that help her become a professional dancer later in life?

When it was finally free time, Kari and her friends, Mandy and Liza, worked on a puzzle in the corner of the classroom. This puzzle pictured a beach scene—exactly where Kari wished she were, playing on the sand with her family.

"Now that swimming is over, I need something to do." Liza gathered the blue water pieces. "My mom says I have too much energy."

Mandy nodded. "That's for sure." She looked at Kari. "Last time she stayed at my house, before you moved here, Liza scared my parents."

"That was the gummy bears. Sugar makes me wanna dance." Liza wiggled in her seat.

"Hey, that's what I'm doing! Dance." Kari sorted through the pieces for anything that looked like puffy white clouds.

"Where?" Mandy sounded interested.

"A dance school near here. My mom heard about it." Kari smiled. "I can't wait."

"Look at this!" Liza stood and did a spin move and a high kick. But she accidentally kicked the table leg. "Oh, no!" She grabbed her right foot and hopped around. "Ow!"

Kari covered her mouth. "Are you okay?"

"Typical Liza. Too much energy." Mandy kept her focus on the puzzle. She'd seen this before.

"Gee, thanks, Mandy." Liza limped back to her seat. "Anyway. I do dance at my church. Mostly on Saturdays. We learned that move last week. Only there wasn't a table leg in the way."

Mandy crossed her arms and stared at the puzzle. "Too many sand pieces."

They all agreed. So they put the puzzle back in the box.

Liza crossed her arms. "Know what I'm most excited about?"

"What?" Mandy looked happy just to be done with the puzzle.

"Basketball." Liza was on her feet again. She dribbled an invisible ball and shot it into an invisible hoop. "Swish! Three points!"

Kari turned to Liza. "The school has a team?"

"We are the team. The whole class." Liza placed the puzzle box back on the game shelf.

"Wait." Kari's heart skipped a beat. "What do you mean?" She hadn't heard about this. Basketball was definitely not her thing.

Liza returned to her spot and sat down with Kari and Mandy. "In PE yesterday. Didn't you hear Mr.

Stone? He said we start the basketball unit tomorrow."

"Oooh." Mandy clapped her hands. "I'm a basketball champion. You may not have known that."

The bell rang and it was time for lunch. While she ate her peanut butter sandwich, Kari laughed at the jokes and kept up with the conversation. But the uneasy feeling in her stomach only grew. How could she play basketball in front of Liza and Mandy—especially when Mandy was a champion? And what about the rest of her class? They were probably all good at basketball.

This was Indiana, after all. Her dad and Luke said this was basketball country.

When lunch was over, Kari felt a nudge in her side from Liza. "What's wrong with you, Kari? You look sick."

"I'm nervous. About basketball." Kari took a deep breath. The girls were still sitting at their lunch table. "Maybe I can miss school. I think Ashley did that once to get out of something. I could ask her how she did it."

"Did it work?" Mandy sounded too interested. Kari didn't blame her. Who wouldn't want a sick day?

"No." Kari sighed. "Mom saw right through it. Still. It could be worth a shot."

"The only shot happening around here is this one." Liza stood and made another pretend jumper. "Come on, girls. Let's go outside. Basketball is easy. I'll show you."

When they were on the recess yard, Liza took a red, white, and blue basketball from the cart. She dribbled it without looking. "Keep your eyes up when you dribble. That's the first rule." She pointed at Kari. "Your turn."

Kari shook her head. "I don't want to."

"Come on, Kari!" Liza waved her over. "I'll teach you."

Mandy and Kari stood and followed Liza to one of the three basketball hoops.

"Spread out." Liza motioned for the girls to have some space between them. "Watch me." She dribbled to the basket, circled the pole, and dribbled all the way back to the girls.

"Nice!" Mandy clapped. "My turn! Remember, I'm a champion."

"Okay." Liza tossed the ball to Mandy. "Prove it."

Mandy set off with great confidence, but a few feet toward the hoop, the ball hit her foot and spun toward the neighboring court. "Oops." Mandy ran after the ball. When she was back at her spot, she grinned at Liza and Kari. "Even champions can get rusty."

"True." Liza clapped for their friend. "Make it count, Mandy. Come on."

This time as Mandy went toward the basket, Liza leaned in closer to Kari. "See how she dribbles it? In rhythm? Kinda like a dance?"

Mandy returned and tossed the ball to Kari.

Her heart pounded in her chest and her sandwich sat high in her stomach. Kari looked at Liza. "I'd rather not."

"You have to!" Liza linked arms with Mandy. "We start tomorrow."

She had a point. Kari took a deep breath and bounced the ball to the ground. When it came up, she slapped it hard, but after only three dribbles the ball was way out in front of her. She ran after it, but it was no use. Every dribble moved it further away.

"You got it, Kari!" Liza shouted at her.

Mandy clapped and cheered as well. "Run faster!"

Faster? Kari thought. Was that the way to win at this? Kari doubled her effort, smacking the ball to the ground and running after it faster and faster and faster until the ball was so far ahead, Kari was dribbling nothing but air. She almost fell, but she caught herself.

Kari ran after the ball and brought it back to her friends. "See? I can't do it."

Liza took the ball. She dribbled it a few times like she could do it in her sleep. "Hmm," Liza said. "You just need to practice. And we will have plenty of time to do that in PE." She smiled at Kari. "Soon you won't be terrible at basketball. I really believe that."

"Yes." Mandy nodded. "You'll be a champion like us in no time." She grinned at Liza. "Right, pal?"

"Right." Liza high-fived Mandy. The two of

them were basketball princesses, apparently.

Once they were back at their desks, the idea of playing basketball with her classmates tomorrow made Kari's stomach hurt. Ms. Nan stood at the front of the room with a stack of papers. Last week they had written a paper about what they wanted to be when they grew up. After much debate and worry, Kari finally wrote about being a dancer.

Maybe this assignment would be better.

"Listen up, class!" Ms. Nan sounded giddy with excitement. "I am thrilled to introduce our new unit. In the next few weeks, we will study nature. Exploring sediment, species, and the way our ecosystem works."

Nature. *Hmm,* Kari thought. She enjoyed nature most of the time. Pretty trees and colorful flowers and fresh air. That sort of thing.

"And something else!" Ms. Nan held up some sort of packet. "You knew this was coming. Two words: science camp!" Their teacher smiled even bigger.

Kari's mouth went dry. Science camp? Like . . . the one Ashley had been talking about?

"As you know," Ms. Nan explained, "it's a long-standing tradition that grades five and six from Bloomington Elementary School attend science camp every fall. Just before the snow hits." She paused. "Who remembers science camp last year?"

Nearly everyone raised their hand.

Of course, Kari had just moved here, so she hadn't been. And now she couldn't believe it. Was Ashley right? Would they make friends with wild bears? Could there actually be a volcano somewhere in the Indiana wilderness?

Now Ms. Nan was passing out a packet to each student. Just like the one Ashley got. Their teacher was still beaming. "The trip will consist of four days and three nights in cabins. There will be challenges and assignments to complete during the day." Ms. Nan looked around. "And best of all, we will work together."

A boy named Curtis raised his hand. "A kid in my class last year saw a bear. Maybe we should bring food in case we see one, too."

Ms. Nan's smile fell off. "I do not expect to see bears this time around, Curtis." She exhaled. "But if we do, we will definitely not feed them."

A shiver ran down Kari's arms. *Oh, no.* If someone saw a bear last year, that meant Ashley was right. They might actually see wild bears. But making friends with them was clearly out of the question. But would there be safety gear? Protection against bears? Kari shivered again.

A few desks away, Liza hung onto every word about science camp. But Mandy slouched in her chair and raised her hand. "Ms. Nan, is science camp optional? I wasn't a big fan last year."

"It's up to your parents, but no, Mandy. It is not." A serious expression came over their teacher's face. "This is part of school, boys and girls."

Kari felt her heart sink. Just what Carly had said. Science camp wasn't an adventure. It was school. Maybe her parents would let her stay home. She tried to picture convincing them that she shouldn't go to camp. Because of the bears, of course.

She frowned. That might not be easy.

"I heard there are new cabins." Darla raised her hand from the front row "Do the new cabins have televisions?" She smoothed her hand over her plaid skirt. "I'm wondering about the amenities."

A few kids giggled under their breath.

"No." Ms. Nan kept a straight face. "The new cabins are just . . . cabins. No television or coffee-makers. No amenities." She took a moment. "This is a time to mix with nature."

Kari stared at her copy of the packet. She still couldn't believe this. Science camp? Really? Cute cartoon photos covered the front page, pictures of trees and birds and worms. Also, there was a list of information. *Home-cooked meals, campfire stories, exploring, science experiments. The adventure of a lifetime!*

Kari stared at the words. The trip would be nothing of the sort.

Ms. Nan went on. "Starting tomorrow we will study soil and sediment, along with the layers that make up the earth. At science camp we will see real-life examples of everything we've learned."

When school was over for the day, Kari walked in silence beside Liza and Mandy.

Finally, Liza spoke up. "Science camp is the best." Liza smiled at Kari and Mandy. "I can't wait. Last year I caught a salamander." She held her hand up as if she had the little guy in her palm. "He had the cutest eyes."

"Well . . ." Mandy's tone sounded less enthusiastic. "My older brother had something scary happen to him at science camp. A few years ago."

"What happened?" Kari looked at Mandy. "Did he get lost in the woods?"

"No." Mandy still looked worried. "But he did fall into a stream and hurt his ankle." Mandy zipped up her hoodie. "And then he got eaten by like a hundred mosquitoes."

"Eaten?" Kari felt her stomach drop. Could a person get eaten by mosquitoes?

"That's what my mom said. Sam got eaten up by mosquitoes." She lifted her shoulders a few times. "But he's still here. So, he didn't get eaten up all the way."

Liza put her hand on her hip. "He had a hundred mosquito bites?"

"Okay. Fine." Mandy rolled her eyes. "Maybe more like twelve. But he said it felt like a hundred." Mandy walked more slowly, clearly distracted by the memory. "Just make sure you bring bug spray."

Kari forced a smile. "Wonderful." She wanted to be excited. But she was too afraid. Bears and mosquitoes? Cabins alone in the woods?

Between science camp and basketball tomorrow, today was a doozy.

Mom waited for Kari and her siblings outside in the family van. Today she was taking them shopping, so they weren't riding the bus. Once they pulled out onto the busy road, Ashley and Erin and Luke all started talking about their days. Kari kept the news about science camp to herself.

Today had turned out very differently than she had hoped. Kari pulled her journal and a pencil from her backpack. Then, even with the bumpy ride, she began to write.

> Hi, it's me again. Today was a bad news day. Not only are we doing a basketball unit, but we are going to science camp. I don't want to do either of those. I wanted an adventure, but not one that included mosquitoes or dribbling basketballs.

She thought for a minute.

And what about the bears? I'll have to talk to Dad about that, because if science camp is too dangerous, he just might let me stay home. More later.

Kari closed her journal and sat back in her seat. Her eyes turned to the window. Today, even the thought of her upcoming dance lesson wasn't enough to make her feel good. She had too much to worry about and she didn't want to think about tomorrow. Because of basketball, and something else.

Tomorrow would take her one day closer to the wild bears.

5

Bo of Many Colors

ASHLEY

Ashley had nothing to wear to church that night. There were twenty-eight items on her bed, but still she had nothing. She sifted through the pants and jeans and sweaters and shirts. *Impressive*, she thought. She actually did have a lot of clothes.

Just nothing to wear.

Mom had not approved of any of her outfits so far. Nothing appropriate for Wednesday night church. And Ashley was on her third try.

She had started with her Wendy costume from her class's Peter Pan presentation. The Wendy slippers and blue dress were so beautiful. They always made her feel like the Queen of Neverland.

With a great deal of sureness, Ashley had slipped into them and floated down the stairs, twirling and singing. "I won't grow up . . . I won't grow up. I don't want to go to school . . . I don't want to go to school." By then she had waltzed into the kitchen. "Here it is, Mother. My Wednesday night church outfit." She held out her arms, "Ta da!"

Mom had taken one look at Ashley and raised her eyebrows. "Definitely not." She had been putting away the dinner leftovers. "You need real clothes for church. Not a costume. Please." Mom had nodded toward the stairs. "Go back up. And go quick. We're running late."

Next, Ashley had found a shiny leotard from her gymnastics class. The shiny rainbow-colored outfit seemed perfect for church. Like something a Bible character might wear. Definitely. But when she stepped back into the kitchen, Mom shook her head.

"Really, Ashley?" Mom had frowned. "No costumes. Please."

Ashley had tried to sell her mother on the idea. "See? It's not a real costume. It's meant for moving around."

"Exactly." Mom shook her head. "A leotard is for the gym. Please, Ashley, you know what people wear to Wednesday night church. Can you just put on jeans or a dress?"

"I could . . . yes." Ashley had paused and tapped her right foot. "But I think this would be better. Especially during the music part of church. I could be more flexible to dance and move around. You know. If the moment called for it." She had twirled and clapped, acting out one possibility. "Perfect, right?" Ashley propped herself on the counter and kicked both legs out behind her. "See?"

"No. I do not see." Mom wasn't smiling. "Go up and get dressed, Ashley. This is your last chance. Otherwise I'll come up and pick something for you." Mom checked her watch. "Kids. John . . . let's go." As she said Dad's name, he entered the kitchen adjusting his tie.

"I'm ready." Dad always dressed nice for church. Even on Wednesdays, when everyone met in small groups and things were more casual.

"Do you like my outfit, Dad?" Ashley had put

66

her hands in front of her, displaying the leotard and sweater.

"Looks great!" Dad grinned.

"John." Mom threw her hands in the air. "She can't wear that. I already told her to change."

"Oh. Ashley." Her father raised his eyebrows at her. "If your mother said to change, you better listen to her."

"Yes, Dad." Ashley hung her head and pivoted out of the kitchen and back upstairs.

That was ten minutes ago.

Now she was staring at the clothes on her bed. But nothing popped out quite like the Wendy costume and leotard.

Kari stepped into the room they shared and stared at Ashley. "Why are you dressed for gymnastics?" She sat on her bed and laced up her shoes.

"I wanted to wear my Wendy costume." Ashley frowned. "But Mom said to change, so I thought this was next best."

For a moment, Kari just stared at her. "For *church*?"

Ashley huffed. "I know. I know."

Kari wore dark blue jeans, a white sweater, and white sneakers. Perfect, like always, Ashley thought. Kari smiled at Ashley as she ran out of the room. "Just wear something normal. But hurry! We're leaving."

Ashley grabbed normal jeans and a normal sweater. She dressed in those normal clothes and tied up her normal shoes. She caught a glance in the mirror as she left. *Not bad,* she told herself. Not Wendy . . . but not bad.

Ashley Baxter made 'normal' look good.

On the way to church, Mom turned around and looked at Ashley. "Thanks for changing."

"You're welcome." Ashley remembered to smile. "But you always say people should come as they are to church. God doesn't care how we look or what we've done." Ashley tugged at her seatbelt. "So why couldn't I wear my Wendy dress?"

"Well . . ." Mom paused. "There's a time and a place for everything."

"Like I wouldn't wear my talent show outfit in the pool?" Kari giggled from her seat between Ashley and Brooke.

"Exactly." Their mom looked satisfied. She faced the front window again.

"Unless tonight was the Christmas play, right?" Ashley did want to get this point across. "Cause then people dress in all kinds of costumes. Wise men. Shepherds. Cows. Wendy from Peter Pan." Ashley looked out the window. *Yes, that's it,* she thought. Maybe this Christmas she could be Wendy in the pageant.

Later that night, Ashley sat at a table with Landon and Elliot and Natalie. Church was extra-fun with her everyday classmates also in her Wednesday night church class. The teacher, Miss Diane, was finishing up a lesson.

The last lesson on Noah.

"And so the rainbow"—Miss Diane pointed to a big colorful rainbow on the chalkboard—"represents God's promise to Noah and his—"

"What promise?" A kid blurted out. "I want to know about this promise." He hadn't been paying attention last week, apparently.

"Okay." Miss Diane's voice was springy and joyful. "The promise that God would never flood the earth again, the way He did when Noah built the ark." She didn't wait for the boy to interrupt her again. "And that, class, is the story of Noah."

Which reminded Ashley . . . She raised her hand. "Miss Diane?"

"Yes, Ashley?" The teacher looked her way.

"Something's been bothering me since we learned about Noah." Ashley folded her hands on her desk. "Why did he let snakes on the boat?"

"What?" Miss Diane looked confused.

"You know." Ashley stood and moved her hands in a snake-like fashion. "Two by two. But why snakes? Noah should've left them off."

"Well. God had a reason." Miss Diane's answer wasn't a real answer. Ashley could tell. It was kind of a because-I-said-so" answer. Which Ashley thought was probably an adult's way of saying, *I don't know and let's move on.*

"What about coyotes?" the same kid from earlier blurted out. "Why coyotes? A coyote ate our cat last week."

"Oh, dear." Miss Diane looked nervous now. She squinched her eyebrows together. "That's terrible."

"It was." The boy looked like he wanted to share the details. "We came out the next morning and only the tail and ears were left."

"Okay." She motioned for the kid to sit back down. "That's all. Let's . . . let's move on."

"Don't you think it would've been better if the coyotes drowned in the flood." The boy wasn't giving up. "Because I think so."

"And the snakes." Ashley nodded. "I've never met a nice snake. Snakes can kill you, you know."

Miss Diane's jaw dropped. "Um . . . I cannot explain why God kept the coyotes and snakes on the ark. That's why God is God, and I am not." She clasped her hands and sighed. "Class, we are almost out of time. But next Wednesday we are going to talk about the story of Joseph!" She looked relieved to move past Noah. "Who knows something about Joseph?"

A quiet girl with braids and glasses raised her hand. "He was engaged to Mary."

"True. Yes." Miss Diane looked a little frazzled. "I'm actually talking about a different Joseph. From the *Old* Testament."

"He was the writer of the Ten Commandments?" Another boy raised his hand. "Right?"

"No . . . no, that's not Joseph. Also, God wrote the Ten Commandments. And *Moses* delivered them to the people." Miss Diane's look said she was done taking guesses from the students. "Joseph was a dreamer. He was a young man with a beautiful coat of many colors and he went through a number of trials. We'll learn all about it next week."

A goat of many colors? Ashley listened harder. What could that possibly mean? Ashley had so many questions, but Wednesday night church was over. The whole way home she thought about Joseph's goat. Who painted it? Was the goat born that way? Or did it change over time? Was it a Billy goat? Or a fainting goat?

The next morning very early before school, when her siblings were still asleep, Ashley woke up and moved to the living room floor. Sometimes she woke up early like this. And when she did, it was time for petting Bo.

If only she had her own goat of many colors. She peered out the window. They definitely had room for one in the backyard. That's when it hit her. The most brilliant idea ever. She could paint Bo!

She grabbed her sketchbook and drew up her idea! The drawing showed Bo looking very excited for this experiment. In the picture, she added bowls all around Bo, each with coloring in it. Jell-O coloring. Yes, that was it! The sketch gave her confidence that she could pull this off in real life.

"Come here, Bo!" She walked to the pantry and found a few boxes of Jell-O. Red and green and blue. "Let's go . . . come on, boy!"

For extra privacy, Ashley headed far out into the backyard with three bowls of water and the Jell-O packets, and got right to work because time for school was coming. A dash of blue, a splash of green, a bit of red. She mixed each bowl and then, using one of her paintbrushes, she applied the color to Bo's white hair.

He seemed to like it. He stood there, frozen, his tail between his legs.

"It's okay, buddy." Ashley patted his head. "When I'm done, you will look fabulous."

But within a few minutes, the Jell-O started to get bouncy, which made it more difficult to paint on Bo.

Ashley's hands had more color than Bo's hair. It was literally a sticky situation.

Brooke slid the glass door open and stepped outside. "Ashley!" she called out across the yard. Then she hesitated a moment. "Ashley? You have to get ready for school. What are you doing?"

"Just a minute." Ashley yelled back at her sister. She walked slowly back to the porch with Bo at her side, "Maybe," she whispered, "I should have used markers."

The closer Ashley and Bo got to the back of the house, the more shocked Brooke looked. "What . . . what did you do to Bo?" She ran to their dog and kneeled down near him. Then she looked up at Ashley. "He looks awful."

"In my defense . . ." Ashley pushed her toe around the grass. "At least I didn't use real paint."

"Why?" Brooke stood and stared at her. "Why did you want to paint Bo?"

"Because." Ashley felt sure of herself. "I wanted my own goat of many colors."

"What?" Brooke looked confused.

"Like Joseph." Ashley wiped her multicolored hands on the grass. It didn't help. "You know, in the Bible."

A few seconds passed, then Brooke closed her eyes. "Ashley. It was a *coat* of many colors. Not a *goat*. Joseph wore a *coat* of many colors."

"A coat." Ashley nodded, picturing it. "That actually makes more sense."

Brooke laughed. "Why would Joseph have a multicolored goat, anyway?"

"You know"—Ashley patted Bo on his sticky green head—"I was wondering the same thing."

Just then, Dad and Luke came around the corner from the front yard. Luke had a basketball under his arm. As soon as they saw Bo they stopped in their tracks.

"Ashley!" Dad hurried over. "What did you do?"

"It's a long story." Ashley covered her face. Then she explained the story to their father. By the time she finished, he was laughing. Luke was, too.

"Hose him off." Dad touched a red streak on Bo's side. "Before he attracts ants. Then you need to get ready for school."

"Yes, Dad." Ashley felt herself relax. That could've gone a lot worse. She called their dog. "Come on, Bo." Then she took her Bo of many colors to the side of the house and rinsed him off. She giggled as the thick Jell-O bits plopped off Bo's back.

Bo licked at it and he almost smiled. Like on the inside, Bo was laughing, too.

Soon enough Bo was clean again. Wet and a little confused, but clean. Ashley watched her dad and Luke and Brooke playing basketball while she ran her hand over Bo. They played basketball in the morning sometimes.

Ashley stared at her hands. They were still all the colors of the rainbow because of the Jell-O Which she kind of liked.

"You're a good friend, Bo," Ashley said to her dog. She kissed him on the forehead, a slight sweet smell still hung on Bo's fur. Her dog wagged his tail and licked Ashley's face. She felt like maybe he was telling her something. Something she would keep a secret. The fact that he actually quite liked being the goat of many colors.

Even if only for this morning.

6

Helping Hands

KARI

Shivering was part of the Great Depression.

It must've been, because Kari and her friends stood outside their sixth-grade classroom on Thursday morning as the first part of Ms. Nan's lesson on that historic time. And Kari was freezing.

Ms. Nan said she wanted them to experience what the people felt in the bitter cold. Because a lot of people couldn't afford to heat their homes. But the lesson was about more than that, their teacher said.

"The Great Depression was a time when everyone helped each other." Ms. Nan set a large black bag on the ground. "Inside this bag"—she looked at the class—"are enough pairs of gloves for each of you." She paused. "We will return to the classroom when everyone has a pair of gloves. But there's one important rule."

Kari waited. Her shivering was getting worse.

When she had everyone's attention, Ms. Nan pointed to the bag. "The rule is this. You may not get a pair of gloves for yourself."

Thoughts turned in Kari's mind. Why couldn't they get their own gloves? Then the answer hit her! Kari ran to the bag, grabbed a pair of gloves, and took it to Liza. "Go! Get some for Mandy!" Kari pointed. "Hurry!"

Liza slipped the gloves on her hands and hurried to the black bag. She found a pair for Mandy, and then Mandy found one for Kari. All around them, their classmates were doing the same thing. In no time, all the students had warm hands.

Ms. Nan folded her arms in front of herself and grinned. "That's what happens when you help someone else. Everyone wins."

Their teacher ushered them back into the classroom. Kari shivered a few more times. Clearly there was nothing great about the Great Depression. Once inside, Ms. Nan draped a shawl over her shoulders, but it wasn't beautiful like her usual clothing. This shawl was filled with holes. Like it was a hundred years old.

"During the Great Depression, people made do with what they had." Ms. Nan looked around. "Food was scarce and people survived by going without. Sometimes all they had was a few pieces of bread to get through the day." She paused. "Try to imagine that."

Kari tried to picture that, she and her siblings sharing a few pieces of bread with nothing else in the refrigerator. It made her thankful for all they had. So thankful.

Ms. Nan was still explaining that time in history. "The Great Depression happened between 1929 and 1941 and it began in the United States. But eventually it spread across the entire world." Ms. Nan sat on the edge of her desk. "Many banks failed, and jobs were hard to come by. Life was difficult for many people, but it also brought friends and family together."

At least that part sounded good. People coming together.

Ms. Nan reached into a big bag and pulled out a black pot. She held it up. "This is a replica of the sort of iron pot people used during the Great Depression. Often they made big batches of soup to make their meat and vegetables into more of a meal."

Kari did not like soup. Not at all. She raised her hand. "What if people didn't like soup?"

Ms. Nan smiled. "People learned to like it. The soup they ate during the Great Depression was mostly water. It was a way to survive."

"Oh." Kari couldn't imagine life being like that, bread and soup and cold at night. Again the truth of the history lesson made her thankful.

"I think soup is cool," Jason called out. Jason sat in the front row. He was the gold medalist of just about everything school related. "At least they had something." The boy looked around. "Right?"

The other students nodded. They all looked gripped by what they were learning. And grateful the Great Depression had eventually ended. Ms.

Nan held up a photo of men standing on a street corner. "Most men would go out each day looking for any work they could get. Anything to help their families."

"Ms. Nan?" Mandy sat a little straighter. "How did women help out in the Great Depression?"

Their teacher smiled. "I like that you're thinking, Mandy." Ms. Nan nodded. "Women found ways to make money, too. Sewing, cooking, accounting, working in the medical field. Again, whatever they could do to help bring in money for their families."

That answer seemed to make Mandy happy. She sat back in her seat.

"When times got especially tight, there might not have been even soup for people to eat. That's when they would make this." Ms. Nan lifted a block of flat bread from her bag. "This . . . is hardtack. A common food source during the Great Depression." Ms. Nan held the bread up in the air.

It didn't look like actual food. Kari raised her hand again. "How did they make it?"

"Good question, Kari. The women would mix

unleavened flour and water, and then bake it in a stone oven." Ms. Nan knew a lot about this topic. She raised her eyebrows. "It was definitely the sort of bread that never spoiled."

Two ingredients? *No wonder it never went bad,* Karl thought.

Liza raised her hand. "Why is it called hard-tack?"

"Listen." Ms. Nan flicked the bread block with her finger. "It's hard as a rock."

She found a plastic container next to her desk and showed the class. "I have one piece of hard-tack for each of you. Chew carefully." She walked around the circle handing out the biscuits. "Families made this bread when times were extra tight, when there was no money for food. That's how they stayed alive during the Great Depression."

Kari leaned over and whispered to Mandy. "I would've made oatmeal."

"Yeah." Mandy nodded. "Or pancakes."

Liza held her hands in the air. "They couldn't afford that stuff." She shrugged. "I think that's the whole point."

When it was her turn, Kari took a piece from the bin. "Whoa." She tightened her grip on the bread. "It's heavy."

"Yes." Ms. Nan looked around the classroom. "One piece of hardtack could last several days. But it's very heavy."

Kari put the biscuit between her teeth and tried to bite down. Nothing happened. She furrowed her forehead and adjusted the position of the biscuit. Then she bit down again. Still nothing. Ms. Nan wasn't kidding. The thing was rock solid. *Maybe if Ms. Nan gives us a hammer,* Kari thought.

"I can't . . ." Liza tried biting the hardtack as well. "I can't bite through it."

Mandy watched Kari and Liza struggle. "Nope. I can't, either." She handed the biscuit back to their teacher. "I decline."

Kari finally broke through the outer crust and chewed a small bite. The stuff was terrible, but it made her appreciate the people of the 1930s. Trying to survive day after day for their families. Eating this hardtack.

Jason coughed a few times. "Ms. Nan, so you're

telling me they didn't have pizza? Or even a sand-wich? Just these dry things?"

Ms. Nan tightened her shawl around her shoul-ders. "In many cases, yes." She looked at the other students. "The important lesson here, students, is that the Great Depression affected everyone." Ms. Nan took her time. "Men and women alike. Children, too. They had to help out wherever they could. However they could. They saw a need and took care of it."

Mandy raised her hand. "My dad says we have to help wherever we can now, too."

"Yes." Ms. Nan smiled. "We're not that much different from people back then. There is always an opportunity to help others. We just have to pay attention."

Kari liked the thought of helping someone else. Whenever she could. Also, she was glad that she and her family didn't have to worry about the Great Depression.

They didn't have to be cold and tired. And they didn't have to eat hardtack.

Later that day back at home, the weather was a

lot nicer than it had been before. The sun was out, so everything felt warmer than it had for a long time. Kari ran to her room, grabbed her jump rope, and headed for the back door.

That's when she saw Erin.

Her youngest sister sat at the kitchen table, her head down. All around her were art supplies. Ripped-up paper, glitter, pipe cleaners, cardboard, crayons. The area was a mess.

"You okay, Erin?" Kari paused. Her right hand was on the door, ready to open it. Ready to go outside and do what she wanted to do.

Erin lifted her head. "I guess." She didn't sound very convincing.

Kari winced. She so badly wanted to go outside. But if Erin needed her . . . She remembered what Ms. Nan had said earlier. *There is always an opportunity to help others, we just have to pay attention.* Kari closed her eyes and exhaled. She took her hand off the door handle and walked to her sister.

"Tell me, Erin." Kari sat in the chair beside her. "What's wrong?" She put her hand on her sister's shoulder.

Tears built up in Erin's eyes. "I can't figure out my shadow box project."

"Shadow box?" Kari rummaged through the materials on the table. "What for?"

"We're learning about the rainforest. We have to make a shadow box with a certain animal from that place."

"Where's Mom?" Kari glanced toward the kitchen. Usually, their mother helped them with big projects.

Erin sniffed. "Mom's helping Brooke study for a test. Up in Brooke's room." Erin looked pathetic. "Mom said . . . she'd help me later. But what if I run out of time? I just really need help."

Her words stayed with Kari. Erin needed help. Suddenly she remembered what Ms. Nan said about helping each other. Her attitude shifted right there on the spot. "Okay . . . I'll help you!"

Erin hesitated. "Are you sure you don't mind?"

"Not at all." Kari pulled the stack of green paper closer. "What's your animal?"

"The poison dart frog." Erin reached for a fact sheet about the animal with a photo attached. "I want to make the blue and black kind. And a yellow and black one."

"Good idea." Kari reached for blue, and black, and yellow paper. "You make the frogs. I'll help with the vines. Then we can color the inside of the box before we start putting the whole thing together."

Erin smiled. "I like it." She glued the strips of black onto the blue body of the frog. "How's this?"

"Great. I love it." Kari liked this. Nothing outdoors would've been as fun as helping her littlest sister.

"Riiiibbit!" Erin held up the first finished frog. "Look at him. He's cute." She stared at the paper frog.

"He is cute." Kari handed her sister half of the strips of brown and green and a glue stick. "Okay. Glue these to the top of the inside of the box. So they hang down like vines."

"This will look so good." Erin bounced a little in her seat.

And half an hour later the shadow box looked just perfect.

Kari helped Erin clean up the mess, and then Kari grinned at her sister. "Let's go jump rope before dinner."

Erin stood up and stretched. "Great idea."

A nice feeling filled Kari's heart as she and Erin played outside together.

She may not have baked hardtack or served as a nurse for injured soldiers in a war, but Kari had done what Ms. Nan said. She had seen a need and stepped in to do what she could. Not only did she help Erin, but Kari had fun doing it. Because helping other people makes everyone feel better.

Before bed, Kari pulled out her journal and filled in an entry for the day.

Hi, it's me, Kari. After school I helped Erin. I wasn't going to at first, but I remembered that it's important to help out when you see a need. That's what they did in the Great Depression. And it's what God wants us to do, too. Plus, helping Erin make a shadow box distracted me from you know what . . . science camp.

Kari turned off her lamp and rolled over on her side. She exhaled, a joyful sigh. Ms. Nan was right. When you help out, something very special happens.

Everyone wins.

7

Saving Stew

The school gym buzzed as everyone waited for the assembly to start. Shouts, laughs, and chatter echoed throughout the space, the students' voices bouncing all around the room. Ashley sat on the floor with her class talking with Elliot and Natalie.

Everyone sat crisscross applesauce. That's what Mr. Garrett called it. He said that whenever he wanted the class to sit. Ashley wished he chose something else to call it. Because anytime they sat down on the floor, Ashley craved applesauce.

Maybe he should call it crisscross stroganoff. Ashley definitely didn't like stroganoff.

"Do you guys miss Peter Pan?" Natalie sighed. "I do."

"You do?" Ashley's mouth dropped open. "You were so nervous about that though. You said you were camera shy!"

"I was. But then being on stage, under the lights . . . " Natalie started to daydream. "And in my Tinker Bell costume. Well, I guess I changed my mind."

Ashley imagined herself in front of the school as Wendy. "I miss it, too, Natalie."

As more students filed into the gym, the noise grew. Ashley sat a little taller, stretching her neck to see who else was around her. She turned to her left and saw Landon. He was talking with his friends.

"Landon!" Ashley shouted over the noise, before ducking to hide between Natalie and Elliot. But she snuck a peek, spying on Landon. She could see him looking in every direction.

"He's trying to find who said it." Natalie giggled.

Ashley popped up again. This time she used a deep voice. "Landon!" Once more, she ducked down in between her friends.

"You got him again. He's searching for someone," Elliot whispered.

Ashley covered her mouth so Landon wouldn't see her laughing. She sat up again and looked at Landon. His face was very confused.

She pitched her voice very high. "Landon. Landon Blaaaaake!" This time she didn't hide. She watched Landon look around the gym once more. This time, a smile spread across his face. He was liking the game. Using her normal voice, Ashley shouted one last time. "Landon!"

Landon locked eyes with Ashley. "It was *you*!" he yelled over the noise.

Ashley shrugged and smiled. "I gotcha!"

Landon laughed and then he came and sat by Ashley. "You're funny."

"Well. I'm also an artist." Ashley wanted to be clear about that.

"Okay." Landon laughed. "I remember your zoo giraffe. You're an artist. Definitely." He grinned at her. "But you're still funny."

"Attention third, fourth and fifth graders." The voice of their principal, Mr. Bond, echoed through the gym, louder than any of the chatter. "Let's settle down please."

The gym grew quiet

"First, I'd like to congratulate everyone on your recent very successful talent show." The principal stood at the front of the gym. "Very good job, students." He began to clap, and the place erupted in lots of applause.

Ashley clapped a little longer than everyone else. Because her performance as Wendy deserved it.

"Now." Mr. Bond held up his hand. Again, the gym became quiet. "In December, a few weeks from now, we will be giving out character awards."

"This is perfect for me," Natalie whispered. She sat on the other side of Ashley. "I always win these."

Ashley smiled at her friend. Natalie probably did win character awards. But probably not for humility.

Principal Bond was explaining the situation. "We will honor several students each week in December. There will be awards for hard work, honesty, friendship, cooperation and thinking of others."

Hmm, Ashley thought. *I'm good at all those things.*

The principal gave a few other announcements and dismissed them to their classrooms. The entire way back, Elliot and Natalie talked about the awards. But Ashley didn't say anything. She was too busy thinking how if she did win one, she would not only be the queen of Field Day, but also queen of the whole school!

That afternoon, Luke went fishing with their dad. Ashley wanted to go, but their father said maybe next time. Today was just for Luke.

So, Brooke and Erin did homework at the kitchen table, and Kari read in the living room. It was too quiet inside. And even though Ashley had math problems to conquer, she was too excited to focus so she found Mom out back.

"I'm figuring out a plan to win, Mother." Ashley paced in front of what used to be the summer vegetable garden. Now it was dead plants, and her mom was pulling them out and putting them into a bucket.

Mom smiled at her. "It sounds very exciting, Ashley."

"Yes." Ashley spun around. "All I have to do is not fall asleep in class and maybe help Mr. Garrett without being asked. I need to be nice to everyone and not complain and tell the truth and boom! I win!" Ashley walked up to her mother. "Then I'll be queen of the school."

"Ashley . . ." Mom sat back on her heels. She wore gardening gloves, and she was using a metal claw-type tool. "Awards aren't the reason we do those things."

"They aren't?" Ashley put her hands on her hips. "Why then?"

Mom laughed. "Cause being a good citizen, showing kindness to others and offering to help . . . that's part of being a Baxter. It's the way God wants us to behave."

"Oh." Ashley slowly dropped to the ground. "Then . . . can I help you, Mother?" She reached for the garden claw. "I believe I could use a little character practice."

"Okay." Mom pointed to a bunch of brown vines. "Those are dead. Try to break them up."

Ashley liked the sound of that. Dead things

needed to go. She dragged the claw against the vines until they were extra dead.

At least it seemed that way.

Before she could completely tear apart the dead things, Luke's voice came from the back door. "We're home! I was the best fisherman on the lake today!"

"Luke did great!" Dad's voice sounded excited.

"Did you catch anything?" Mom stood and turned to the back door. Ashley did the same. She still had the claw in her hand. She could think of other things that tool would be useful for.

Dad and Luke walked down the back porch stairs, fishing poles in their hands. Dad carried his tackle box. They set their things down and Dad released a long sigh. "Luke, tell them about your fish!"

"I caught two really big ones." Ashley's younger brother held his hands out as wide as his shoulders. Then he brought his hands in a little more. "And three small ones."

"Sounds like you'll be making dinner." Ashley grinned at Luke. "Nice work. We're like a wilderness family now."

97

"No." Dad did a quiet laugh. "We released the fish back into the lake."

"Yeah, and we watched them swim back to their families." Luke looked proud of himself.

So much for dinner, Ashley thought. "I thought the whole point was to eat them."

"Not always." Dad washed his hands under the hose pipe. Then he dried them on his jeans and grinned at Ashley. "Sometimes fishing is a sport."

"Hmm." Ashley looked at Luke. He was messing with the tackle box. "Well, then, Luke. You win the gold medal for today's fishing competition."

Luke laughed. "You're always giving me gold medals, Ashley."

"Imaginary gold medals." Ashley raised her hands. "To get you ready for the real kind one day."

When Mom had collected the claw and put her gardening tools away, and when they were all back inside, Luke told the others about his day on the lake.

Brooke set her homework down. "Dad? How come you didn't take us fishing?" She crossed her arms.

"Well, Brooke." Dad removed his jacket and hung

it over a chair. "Today was special time with just Luke. But we're going as a family tomorrow, remember? Our big adventure!"

Ashley tapped Brooke's shoulder. "To be fair, Dad, Brooke and I like fishing more than Luke."

"No way!" Luke's eyebrows sunk low. "No one likes it more than me."

"It's not a competition." Brooke giggled. "I'm just glad we all get to go tomorrow."

"Yes!" Erin stood from her place on the sofa. "It will be so fun! Plus, now I'm old enough to learn how to fish."

"True." Dad nodded. "And Lake Monroe is perfect now. Before winter sets in."

Mom washed her hands in the kitchen sink. "We've all been looking forward to our family adventure."

"Exactly! I can't wait." Dad clapped his hands together. "Our fishing and hiking adventure starts in the morning!"

"Yes!" Ashley jumped around like a kangaroo. She bounced across the dining room into the kitchen and then into the living room, where Kari was still reading. She'd been quiet this whole time.

"We're going fishing, Kari. Tomorrow morning!"

Kari wrinkled her nose. "No thanks. I'll stay here and finish my book."

"What?" Ashley stopped jumping. She walked over to her sister. "Fishing will get you ready for science camp. Did you think about that?"

That was apparently not what Kari wanted to hear. She did a thumbs-down sign and kept reading.

"Fine." Ashley hopped back to the kitchen, a little less enthusiastically. That had been one of her spelling words this past week. Enthusiastically. Ashley was still learning how to spell it, but she definitely knew what it meant.

It was how she lived every day! Audacious and enthusiastic.

Especially with two adventures ahead—fishing and science camp.

The night passed extra-slow, but finally it was the next morning. And the whole family—even Kari—was on the dock of Lake Monroe surrounded by fishing gear. Mom unfolded a few chairs.

"I'm a fish-fish-fishergirl, that is what I'll be." Ashley had made up a song on the way to the lake. "Queen of the school and queen of all I see."

Luke danced a little jig near the edge of the pier. "Fish-fish-fisherman, this is where I stand . . . king of the lake, and king of the land!"

"Good job, Luke. Perfect!" Ashley gave her brother a thumbs-up. Then she adjusted her hat. She wore a bucket hat today with several pins and bait pieces attached. It used to belong to Dad.

Now Ashley began dancing, too. Sort of an old-fashioned dance where she folded her arms and kicked her feet out one way, then the other. A Russian dance, perhaps. "All together now." She waved at her siblings. "I'm a fish-fish-fishergirl, that is who I am. But you'll never catch me eating . . . green fishes or green ham!"

The other kids were finding chairs and watching the show. Dad worked to put a worm on one of the hooks and Mom was sorting through the cooler.

"I'm a fish-fish-fisherman . . ." Luke was singing louder now. His dance moves were bigger than before. Big kicks and extra-strong jumps.

101

Later Ashley would admit that Luke had probably danced his way too close to the edge of the pier. But she was so caught up in his joyous song, that she didn't say anything until—

"Fish-fish-fishhhhhh—" Luke went flying over the edge of the dock and into the water. SPLASH!

"Luke!" their mother screamed. She put her hands over her eyes.

All the kids raced to the edge of the pier and Dad got down on his stomach. He reached out one hand to Luke, who was gasping and thrashing around in the lake.

"Help is on the way!" Ashley ran full force across the pier and jumped high in the air. She landed—SPLASH—right next to Luke. The water was freezing. Also, the bucket hat was now over her eyes so she couldn't see. Plus, she was gasping and thrashing around, too. Just like Luke.

Which wasn't really all that helpful.

"Ashley!" Her mother screamed her name next. "Take off the hat!"

Good idea, Ashley thought. She pulled it off and flung it further out into the lake. "G-g-get us outta h-h-here please!" she called out. "Someone h-h-help!"

Both Ashley and Luke could swim. But the water was freezing, and Ashley's clothes felt like bags of cement. That was the problem here.

Dad helped Luke first, and then Ashley, all while Brooke and Kari and Erin stood watching. Their mouths were open like perfect, nice-looking, well-behaved fish.

"S-s-sorry, Dad." Luke shook from the cold. "I g-g-guess I got carried away."

"Yes." Their father sounded stern. "Carried all the way off the dock." He looked at their mom, and Ashley could see a smile trying to break through on his face. "Elizabeth, please get the blankets from the car."

"Wh-wh-whew." Ashley was shivering very hard. "G-g-glad you were thinking ahead, D-D-Dad. Blankets. G-g-great idea."

It took a while, but finally Luke and Ashley were bundled in extra-warm blankets, side by side in two of the chairs. Their shoes were wet, but there was no getting around that. Not without going home. And no one wanted to do that.

"Please . . . just sit there." Dad raised his eyebrows at them. "You can watch today." He left to help Brooke and Kari and Erin with their fishing rods.

Ashley leaned close to her brother, and in her softest singing voice she started again. "I'm a fish-fish-fishergirl . . ."

And Luke—who was her best brother ever—did the slightest small dance moves with the tips of his dripping wet shoes.

The two grinned at each other and settled in as the official audience of the family fishing adventure.

By then Dad had used the longest pole to rescue his old fishing hat. It sat, sort of dejected, near the chairs. Water was still draining off it.

Their dad put his hands on his knees and gestured for the nondancing Baxter children to gather around. "Let's keep our voices low, so we don't scare off the fish. Got it?" He looked at Ashley. "That includes you audience members over there."

"Yes, sir." Ashley did a slight salute. "Quiet as a mouse over here." The others stared at her. "Why are you all looking at me?"

Brooke whispered. "Because sometimes you can be very loud."

"Yes. Okay." She held up both wet hands. "Fair enough."

"Brooke and Kari and Erin . . . you each get a little cup of worms." Dad smiled at the three girls. "I'll help you put a worm on the hook, and show you how to cast it into the water. That's how you'll catch a fish." Dad passed out the worm cups.

Ashley couldn't believe it. She stood. "Over here!" As soon as the loud words came out, she covered her mouth. "Sorry!" she whispered this time. "Over here, please. I'd like a worm cup, too."

"And me!" Luke held out his hand.

"Next time." Dad gave them a serious look. "You'll just watch today. You two need to stay warm."

Ashley plopped back down and linked arms with Luke. "Fine. We will be in fish prison together."

"Yes." Luke laughed very soft. "Fish-fish-fisher prison."

"Exactly." Ashley giggled. "Luke, I like your scent of humor."

Mother stepped closer. "Sense of humor, Ashley. Not scent."

"Pa-taytoes, pa-tawtoes." She shrugged. "Humor can be a scent, Mother. Not sure if you knew that."

Mom laughed and shook her head. Then she joined the actual fisher people at the edge of the dock. There, the show was getting more interesting. Erin looked like she might cry.

"You mean . . . you put the hook right *through* these sweet baby worms?" She frowned. "Poor wormies!"

"That's how it works, sweetheart." Dad patted Erin's head. "You can sit with Ashley and Luke if you'd like." Possibly their father's patients were running out. That could only happen to a father who is also a doctor.

Dad looked at Erin. "Fishing is optional for today's adventure."

"Okay." Erin waved at the worms in her cup. She looked happier now that she didn't have to hook them.

Dad looked at Brooke and Kari. "Fish eat worms anyway. It's the circle of life."

106

"How do we bait the hook?" Brooke apparently didn't care much for worms. She grabbed one and gave it to their father.

This was Ashley's moment. She waved at Erin and talked in an extra-quiet whisper. "Pssst. Over here!"

Her youngest sister hesitated, like she wasn't sure she should mingle with Ashley. Not today, anyway. But while Dad was helping Brooke, Erin brought her cup of worms to Ashley and handed it over. "Look how cute they are."

Ashley moved her fingers through the dirt. The pink worms squirmed through the soil, like they were having the time of their lives. "I think I like worms." She smiled at Erin. "They *are* cute." She picked up one and set it on the palm of her hand. It tickled and wiggled around in a circle.

Next, it was Luke's turn. He took a worm from Erin's cup and held it gently between his fingers. Then he swung it around. "I think this one likes me."

Erin looked nervous. "Dad said you're supposed to just watch."

"We're not fishing." Ashley grinned at Erin. "Also, this is a better morning for these worms than . . ." She looked at Dad and Brooke. "You know. The thing we don't speak of."

Near the edge of the dock, Dad had one poor worm secured to a spiky hook. "Perfect." He grinned at Brooke. Mom and Kari stood nearby watching. "Now we'll cast the hook into the water and see what happens."

Ashley couldn't bear to watch. She picked up her worm and swung it around, same as Luke was doing. She leaned close to the little guy. "Hello, Stewart."

"Stewart?" Erin giggled. "That's a funny name."

"His friends call him Stew." Ashley turned to her sister. "It's a perfectly wonderful name for a worm."

"I like it." Luke, the true professional fisherman, put his worm in the palm of his hand. "My worm is called Nothanks."

"Nothanks?" Ashley was laughing now, too. "Where'd you get that name?"

"Because"—Luke gave the little worm a ride up and down through the air—" 'Nothanks, I don't want to be bait!' That's what he told me."

For what felt like fifty hours, Brooke and Kari fished with their mom and dad. None of them even noticed the worm festival Ashley and Luke and Erin were having back at the chairs.

Just then Dad began walking their way. He held out his hand. "I need those worms, please. We're out of bait."

Ashley began to panic. She couldn't bear to see Stewart smashed onto the hook. He wasn't just any old wiggly worm. He was her friend. "Quick," she whispered to Luke. "Hide the worms!"

Luke dropped Nothanks on the ground near his feet and Ashley slipped Stew down her shirt. "Good luck, boys," she whispered into the cup of dirt. Then she handed it to her father.

"Thank you, Ashley." Dad smiled at the three youngest siblings. "You kids are being very good watchers."

Just then Stew squirmed all the way down to her belly button. Ashley twisted one way, then the other, but she managed to still smile at her dad. "Thank you. We are . . . doing our best."

Next to her, both Luke and Erin had seen what

had happened. When their dad was back with Kari and Brooke and Mom at the edge of the dock, Luke motioned to Ashley. "You can't keep him down your shirt!"

"I know." Ashley stood and flung her blanket off. She pulled her shirt out and Stewart fell, SPLAT, to the ground. Ashley used superfast hands to brush the yuck off her stomach. "Bad idea, Ashley," she told herself. "Very bad idea."

By now, both Stewart and Nothanks looked dried out. They were moving across the dirt much slower than before. "I think they need a swim." Erin peered at the little guys.

"She's right." Luke stood. "I'll take care of them." He held up Stewart. "Say goodbye, Ashley."

She hadn't expected their friendship to end so soon. "Goodbye, Stew. You've been a faithful friend. If you went to my school, you'd win a character award. I just know it."

Again, Erin giggled. "You're my funniest sister, Ashley."

"Thank you." Ashley bowed. She'd been doing that a lot lately. Ever since playing Wendy in the school talent show. Because bows shouldn't just be for the stage.

Ashley remembered Stewart and she felt her smile disappear. "Do good in life, Stew. Make me proud."

"Ashley . . . he needs water." Luke had Nothanks in one hand and Stewart in the other. He walked the worms to the edge of the dock careful not to fall in. Before Mom or Dad or Kari or Brooke could notice, Luke tossed the worms into the lake. Then Luke brushed his hands together, pulled the blanket around his shoulders once more and sat down.

"Swim, Stew," Ashley called out in that direction.

Their mom turned around and looked at her. "What did you say, Ashley?"

"Just . . . practicing my encouragement, Mother." Ashley nodded. "Working on my character awards."

Without the worms, Ashley and Luke and Erin could do nothing more than watch. Another fifty hours later and finally it was time to eat their picnic breakfast. Ashley and Luke were dry enough now, so Dad said they could join in the meal.

Ashley was glad. She hated the thought of starving to death right here on the shores of Lake

Monroe. After breakfast, they were planning to hike the wilderness. Maybe look for buffalo or penguins. Ashley wasn't sure.

So, the adventure wasn't a total loss for Ashley and her youngest siblings.

In all, Ashley and Luke had learned a new song and dance, as well as how not to dance too close to the edge of a pier. Brooke had caught three fish and Kari, two. And the best news, of course, all fish had been safely returned to their lake families.

Ashley just hoped the same was true for Stewart and Nothanks.

8

Lost on Mount Everest

KARI

The hike was just what Kari needed to get ready for science camp.

That's what Kari kept telling herself, during their family picnic breakfast of egg sandwiches on the pier. And by the time Dad gathered up the kids to explain the outing, Kari was actually looking forward to the adventure ahead.

"Most important is that we stay together." Dad looked at Ashley. "That means you, Miss Fisher-girl."

Ashley spread her fingers over her chest. "Me?" Her eyes were wide with shock. "I'm the *last* person you should worry about, Dad."

The other kids tried not to laugh.

Kari put her arm around Ashley's shoulders. "You do have a history of getting lost, Ash. Think about it."

For a few seconds, Ashley looked up to the sky, as if memories of past events were flashing through her head. "Yes." Ashley did a few solid nods. "You have a point." She tipped her head toward their father. "Today, Father, *together* is my favorite word."

"Thank you." Dad chuckled. "We'll be hiking up a few hills and at times the trail will come close to the water's edge." He looked at Luke. "So let's keep our dancing feet on the path."

"Yes, sir." Luke's smile seemed a little nervous. "I'm staying dry the rest of the day!"

"Good." Dad grinned at the group. "Mom and I will take the lead. And if we see anything interesting, we'll point in that direction. Remember"—he lowered his voice—"animals scare easily. So, let's not be too loud."

They made their way to the trail, which was soft dirt with green wild bushes and yellow flowers on either side. Every ten steps or so a towering tree cast cool shade over the path.

"I think I'll paint this place one day." Ashley stopped and studied one of the flowers. "I'll paint this exact trail and these very same flowers and bushy bushes and perfect trees." She spun and smiled at their mother. "And I will give the painting to you, Mother, for your birthday."

Their mom gave Ashley a side hug. "I'd like that very much, Ashley."

"Yes." She nodded. "I thought so."

Kari wasn't sure how she was supposed to compete with that. She held one hand out as they walked. The soft branches of the bushes brushed against her fingers. "Well . . ." She positioned herself on the other side of their mother. "When I'm older I'll write you a story about this place. And I'll talk about this day when we were young, and we took this hike as a family . . . for the first time. And the book will be called *Adventure Awaits* and it will be in all the stores." Kari smiled at Mom. "But you'll know deep in your heart that it's really just for you."

Mom stopped and kissed the top of Kari's head. "I must be the most blessed mother in all the world." She looked at Ashley and then at Kari again. "I can't wait for both those precious gifts. Ashley's painting and your book, Kari."

"Yes." This time Kari nodded. "I thought so."

Brooke and Erin and Luke were up ahead on the trail with their dad. Otherwise, they each would've had to think of a future gift for their mother, too. Just to keep up.

Kari looked back, but the pier where they had started was nowhere in sight. Dad was right about the lake being right off the path. A few steps to the right and they'd be in it. Also, a stream ran along the other side. So, there was water pretty much everywhere.

She would have to include that in her book.

"Look!" Brooke whispered and pointed toward the stream.

The others turned that direction and Kari did a quiet gasp. A mama deer and her baby were standing in a green meadow so close Kari could hear their feet moving in the grass. They were the most beautiful wild animals ever. She held her breath and didn't move.

A squirrel jumped from one branch to the next and hurried down the trunk of a tree. The noise startled the deer and the two darted off, disappearing into the deep, thick layers of trees.

Ashley watched them disappear into the distant woods. "That settles it." She turned to Kari and Mom. "God really is the best artist."

"He is." Mom picked up her pace. "Let's catch up with the others."

The family walked a little further and the trail started to go uphill.

"Okay." Dad faced the group. "This part can be a little tricky. So, watch your step."

"We can pretend we sailed here . . . and we got shipwrecked!" Luke pumped his fist in the air. "And now we have to hike to the top of the tallest mountain before we can get rescued!"

"I like that." Brooke patted Luke's head.

"The tallest mountain . . ." Kari's voice drifted off. Then it hit her. "Mount Everest!"

Kari followed the rest of the family up the hill. After a few minutes, her legs hurt and her lungs felt heavy. This was for sure the tough part.

She imagined something. This wasn't just a hike around Lake Monroe. Now Kari was making her way up the actual Mount Everest. Yes, that was it. Kari had heard about that place in school. Mount Everest was the world's tallest mountain, and it was always freezing cold.

Suddenly her foot slipped and she gasped. Rocks and dust bounced and rolled down the side of the trail. But instead of a million miles down like it would be on Mount Everest, the rocks tumbled down four or five feet. So much for Mount Everest.

"Kari!" Ashley's voice pulled Kari from the daydream. "I was calling you. Are you okay?"

Kari blinked. "Hmm? Oh yeah." She tugged at her jacket sleeve. "Just thinking. This feels like hiking Mount Everest."

"Everest!" Ashley's eyes got really wide. "I was thinking the same thing!"

"I hear there's treasure buried at the top!" Kari's excitement rang in her own voice. Ashley would play along with her. She always did.

"Yes! Treasure!" Ashley gasped. "We have to find it."

"We will." Kari nodded. The others were further up ahead. This adventure was for the two sisters alone. "Keep moving, Ashley! Push through the snow! Stay away from the cliffs!" Kari put her hand on Ashley's shoulder. "No matter how high the mountain gets, don't stop!"

"I won't give up!" Ashley grabbed Kari's hand. "But be careful. There is a snow monster out here somewhere!"

"We'll have to find shelter soon." Kari looked around. The grass had transformed into a snowy white tundra. "This freezing wind hurts my face!"

Ashley pointed up the path. "I see a tent. Up ahead, with the other explorers!"

"What's that?" Kari crouched down. She was breathing fast. "That noise!" Then, as clear as day, Kari could see it. A large, looming, hairy beast of a creature. She covered her eyes. "He must be six feet . . ."

"He's ten feet tall." Ashley screamed. "It's him! The abdominal snowman!"

Kari stood up and blinked. A laugh bubbled up inside her and the snow turned to grass again. "The abdominal snowman? Do you know what abdominal means?"

Ashley threw her arms straight up and stood on her tiptoes. Then she growled, loud and long. "Abdominal snowman, Kari! Come on! That's a snow monster."

The laughter stayed quiet in Kari. "No." She put her hands on her stomach. "Abdominal is when it's from your stomach. Like your abdominal muscles. You mean *abominable*. The abominable snowman."

For a few seconds Ashley said nothing. Just stayed with her arms in the air like a snow monster. Then she dropped them to her sides and raised her chin. "My snowman has very strong abdominal muscles. He is the abdominal snowman, Kari."

Mom stopped and turned around. "Girls, you're falling behind! Come on. Keep up!"

"Yes, Mom." Kari looked at Ashley. "Race you to Dad." Both girls ran their fastest and just like that, they were back with their family. Mount Everest disappeared and they were on the path around Lake Monroe.

In fact, they were at the top of a tall hill.

They could see the whole lake and a world of rolling hills. No one said anything. This place was too beautiful for words.

"This is awesome!" Luke pumped his fist in the air.

Brooke sat down and looked straight out over the vista. "It's amazing."

"Wow." Kari whispered to Ashley. "Better than Mount Everest."

"If you like this . . ." Ashley put her arm around Kari. "Then you're going to love science camp."

A clap of thunder shook the ground.

Dad looked up and they all saw the same thing. Dark, enormous storm clouds moving in fast. "Rain wasn't in today's weather report." He pointed back down the path. "Let's turn around. Maybe we can make it back before it hits."

Erin grabbed Dad's legs. "I'm scared."

He patted her head. "It's okay, Erin. The clouds are still a way off."

They were halfway down the hill when big raindrops started falling. *This is about to be a real disaster,*

Kari thought. Especially since she wasn't wearing a jacket.

Luke stopped and put his face up to the sky. Water bounced off his cheeks and forehead. "Look up when you walk, Kari." He grinned at her. "It's more fun this way!"

"You're right!" Ashley held out her hands and looked straight up. "I'm a fish-fish-fishergirl . . ." She sang the same song from earlier in the day and Luke joined in.

Mom looked nervous. "Kids . . . you can sing. But watch your step. The storm's moving fast."

Kari joined Luke and Ashley, walking hands out, but keeping her eyes on the path.

"What do we do, Mom?" Erin held her hands over her head. "I'm getting wet!"

Mom laughed. "Just enjoy it! I'm with Luke and Ashley and Kari!"

In no time the family made their way down the path, singing Ashley's fisher song and laughing about Luke and Ashley falling into the lake and how Ashley couldn't see with her father's hat on her head. They were all soaked when they reached the car, but they were happy and safe.

On the way home, Kari realized something. She had not expected many things about today—like Ashley's song and Luke falling off the pier. Mount Everest, the view from the top of the trail, and even the rainstorm. She wasn't expecting any of that. But she had enjoyed every minute. Back at the house, Kari found her journal so she could write down everything about the day. Before she forgot.

Hi there. It's me. We took a family adventure to Lake Monroe today, and I learned something. If I'm going to enjoy adventures in my life, I will need a few reminders. Especially with science camp coming up.

So, in this book I'm going to write a list of reminders.

She turned the page and wrote at the top:

Kari Baxter's Reminders for Enjoying Any Adventure

Then she wrote the first two, the ones she'd learned today.

> Expect the unexpected.
> Try new things.

Then she wrote a little more about the morning. Because, after all, a long time from now she was going to write a book about this day. A book for her mom and whoever else wanted to read it.

A book called *Adventure Awaits*.

9

Elliot's Super-Duper Birthday Bonanza

ASHLEY

Ashley looked in the mirror and adjusted her father's fisher hat.

After a million days of waiting, today was finally Elliot's Super-Duper Birthday Bonanza. For her costume, Ashley was going to be an actual fishergirl! She smiled at her rain boots, then she grabbed her fishing pole with no hook.

Because Mom said it would ruin the party if she hooked a party guest.

For his birthday gift, Ashley had made Elliot his very own comic book. It was about Elliot meeting an alien named Al in the woods. The two of them head into town for ice cream, then they meet up with Ashley and Natalie at school and play a long game of four square.

Ashley's favorite part was the pictures. She used wild colors and crazy alien shapes for Al, and she took extra time to bring the story to life until the characters practically jumped right off the page.

One more time she stared at the front cover. It read: *The Excellent Adventures of Al and Elliot.*

She hurried to the car with Elliot's comic book in one hand and Dad's fishing pole in the other. Before getting in, she stopped and smiled at her father. "How do I look?"

Dad nodded. "Super-duper."

Ten minutes later they arrived at the party at the same exact time as Natalie.

Ashley waved goodbye to her dad and hurried over to her friend. "Look at you!" Ashley studied Natalie's costume. "You're a perfect queen, Natalie. I always knew you were royal."

"Thanks." Natalie laughed. "I like yours, too. You're a fisherman!"

"A fishergirl." Ashley crossed her arms. "Because I'm a girl, Natalie. And this morning we went fishing."

They walked up the front porch steps, where Elliot was greeting each friend as they arrived. He was dressed like an astronaut.

"Happy Birthday, Elliot!" Ashley shouted. She wrapped her friend in a huge hug. "You look . . . super-duper!" Ashley stepped back. "Today you are not just an unlikely friend. You are a very good friend."

Through his astronaut mask, Elliot looked like he wasn't sure how to take that. He shrugged.

"You're my best friend, Ashley. So now we're the same." He looked at her. "You're a fisher—"

"Girl! That's right, Elliot." Ashley held up her fishing pole. "I'm a true in-person actual fishergirl!"

Natalie patted Elliot's shoulder. "And you look like a real astronaut."

Elliot held out his hand. "Queen Natalie. I'm glad you could make it!"

Natalie, Elliot and Ashley all laughed.

"Elliot!" A woman's voice rang throughout the house. "Elliot?"

"That's my mom." Elliot stepped inside. "Come on!"

Ashley hesitated. "Oh, no." She winced. "Didn't you tell your parents I was a troublemaker?"

"I said you were a *little bit* of a troublemaker." He laughed. "It's fine. Just . . . be yourself."

The front door opened and a woman stepped out on the porch. She had fiery red, curly hair and she wore a beautiful dark blue sweater.

"Hello, ma'am!" Ashley held out her hand. "It is lovely to meet you. And that sweater is just perfect with your hair color." Ashley waited for a response. Maybe she had overdone it.

Elliot's mom smiled. "Thank you. Good to meet you, Ashley."

Inside, Ashley spotted Landon first. He was dressed as a cowboy, and standing next to him was Chris, wearing a police officer costume. The room was full of doctors, princesses, athletes, and super-heroes. Also, one very happy giraffe.

It was quite the scene.

The living room had been organized into sta-tions. A man walked to the front of the room. He had a large mustache. This must have been Elliot's dad.

"Attention, kids! Welcome to Elliot's Super-Duper Birthday Bonanza." Everyone cheered and screamed until they were shushed by the adults in the room.

Next, Elliot's dad explained the rules of the games and he split everyone into teams. "We will be doing three challenges. A Lego challenge, a drawing challenge, and a footrace challenge."

Four separate boxes of Lego blocks sat on the floor. They were filled with random pieces.

"As you all may know, Elliot loves Legos." Elliot's mom looked proud of her son for that. The woman held up a stopwatch. "Each team has five minutes to put together an original Lego creation. Ready?" She clicked the stopwatch. "Set . . . Go!"

Ashley's team included Natalie, Landon, and Chris. She thought about asking if they could trade teammates, since she didn't really like Chris. But she thought that might not go over well with Elliot's parents.

All at once all the kids were on the floor working with their Lego boxes. "Let's build a house!" Natalie pulled a few of the bigger pieces to the center of the space.

"I like it!" Chris grabbed the largest piece, green and square and perfect for the base of a house.

In no time they had a structure, and Landon and Ashley found the right Lego pieces for windows, a roof and a chimney.

Elliot's mom blew a whistle. "Time!"

"Next up . . ." Elliot's father passed out coloring

pencils and paper. "The Elliot portrait. Five minutes to draw a picture of the birthday boy."

"We'll do good on this one," Ashley whispered to her group. "Because I'm actually an artist." Ashley felt good about this. Whatever they lacked in the Lego challenge, they would make up for in this one.

Ashley did most of the work. She drew Elliot's face and neck and shoulders. Landon and Chris colored in Elliot's shirt. And Natalie drew Elliot's smile, complete with his braces. For the finishing touch, Ashley worked on Elliot's eyes. Her super-duper friend had happy, kind eyes. Like he was always about to do something fun and everyone around him would be included. Ashley had to get them just right. Each person finished their job and the team sat back and looked at their work.

"That's good, Ashley." Chris gave her a thumbs-up.

What was this? Ashley thought. Chris was being nice to her! This really was a special party!

"Time's up!" Elliot's dad shouted above the laughing and chatter. "Last up is the footrace. We will start at the front door and one by one, a team member will run around the house and when they return, they will tag the next teammate."

Elliot's mom raised her hand. "Whichever team finishes first will win!"

"Okay, Chris." Ashley leaned close to her classmate. "We are probably faster than these other people. No offense to them." She glanced at Landon and Natalie. "Right, team?"

Natalie and Landon nodded.

"Okay." Chris crossed his arms "But we'll have to hustle."

"Exactly." Ashley pointed to Chris. "Which is why I should go first. And, Landon, you can go last. In case we need to pick it up."

"I should go last." Chris looked like maybe he was offended. "I'm faster than Landon."

"Well." Ashley raised her eyebrows at him. "If you remember, Chris, I did beat you in a race not that long ago." She patted his shoulder. "But don't worry. I believe in you!"

Chris's face grew red, and Landon seemed to hide a smile. "Fine." Chris tossed his hands in the air. "I'll go after you, Ashley."

"Great." Ashley looked at Natalie. "And you will go third, my friend."

Natalie bounced a few times. "I love going third."

"Perfect." Ashley nodded. She led the group outside, where the first runner from each of the other three teams was lined up along the sidewalk.

"You ready, Ash?" Landon shouted over the group of waiting runners. He gave her a thumbs-up. "You can do it!"

Ashley gave him a thumbs-up, too. Then she bent her knees a few times to warm up her muscles. "Oh yeah." She looked at the runners on either side of her. Then she got into her best running position. "My team is ready to be crowned champion!"

Elliot's dad blew the whistle.

Ashley ran as fast as she could, speeding around the house one foot after the other. A boy named Nick from their class was neck and neck with her. *Focus, Ashley,* she told herself. She nearly slipped in the grass in the backyard, but like the pro she was, she caught herself. Ashley rounded the last corner and tagged Chris.

Elliot's team was the fastest for that lap, but Ashley was close!

Like they had planned, Natalie followed Chris, and Landon ran last. And just like Ashley expected, Landon was faster than everyone in his lap. He was probably the fastest boy in fifth grade.

"I think we need a name," Ashley said after she high-fived Landon. "Like the Speedy Rockets. Something like that."

"We're Team Four, Ashley." Chris laughed. "That's good enough."

"Hmm." Ashley looked at that boy. Just when she thought Chris was getting nicer. "Well, I will call us the Speedy Rockets, all the same."

In the end, the Speedy Rockets only won one of the three competitions. Elliot's team won the drawing event. Which made sense, actually. Because Elliot would know best what he, himself, looked like.

After that, they sang "Happy Birthday" and ate pizza and cake. It was an actual space rock cake that looked like something from Mars. When they were done eating, Ashley picked up the paper plates and forks and headed for the kitchen. Elliot's parents were in there, watching her. "Excuse me . . . where is the trash, please?"

"Here." Elliot's father took a huge plastic bag from a kitchen drawer, fluffed it and gave it to Ashley. "Thank you. That was very helpful of you."

"Yes." Ashley nodded. "I'm working on my character traits." She dumped the garbage in the bag and smiled at the couple. "Plus, I want you to see I'm not a troublemaker. Not really."

"Oh . . ." Elliot leaned forward in his chair. "You're that Ashley." He nodded. "Well, I'm glad to hear that. Elliot thinks you're a lot of fun."

"And funny!" She raised her pointer finger in the air. "I'm sure he told you that, too."

They both laughed, which had to be a good sign. "Yes," Elliot's mother said. "He told us you're very funny."

In the other room they were starting to open presents, so Ashley and Elliot's parents hurried in to see. Ashley took the spot right next to the birthday boy.

After a few presents, she handed him the gift bag with her gift in it. Then she whispered close to his ear. "Mine is the most special. You don't have to say so out loud, though."

"Okay." Elliot pulled the special comic book from the bag and his eyes lit up. He looked right at her. "You made this?"

"I did." Ashley smiled at the other friends in the room.

Elliot flipped through the pages. "You made this for me?" He ran his hand across the cover. *"The Excellent Adventures of Al and Elliot."*

"Yep. Yes, I did." Ashley put her arm around her friend. "You deserve your own comic book."

"I love it." Elliot hugged Ashley. "This is the most best birthday gift ever." He thumbed through the pages, laughing and pointing at all the pictures. He really did seem to like it. And she had cleared her name with Elliot's parents. And that meant that the invitation was exactly right.

This really had been a Super-Duper Birthday Bonanza!

10

Learning Like Luke

KARI

Kari waited till bedtime Sunday night to confess her fears.

When their father came into Kari and Ashley's room to say good night, Kari practically blurted out the truth.

"Dad . . . we started basketball in PE last week. Tomorrow we have to play. Dad, I'm so scared."

"You are?" Dad seemed surprised. "Honey, why?"

Kari bit her lip until she had the right words. "Well . . . I don't want to look silly. Or make a scene. I just don't think I'm good at it."

"Kari . . ." Dad sat on the edge of the bed. "We aren't always good at something right away. And it's important for us to do challenging things. It grows us."

"Dad." Ashley joined the conversation from her bed across the room. "We just signed a pledge. We're trying *not* to grow up, remember?"

"Exactly." Kari sighed. "I'm happy just the way I am."

Dad did a soft laugh. "Girls, when something grows you, it doesn't mean you grow up faster. It means you'll become a more accomplished person. More skilled," he explained. "You may end up liking basketball."

"I'm not so sure, Dad." Kari sat up in bed and looked at her father.

"Listen." He put his arm around Kari. "On my first day as a doctor I was so nervous." Dad raised his eyebrows. "Really."

"You?" Kari couldn't believe it. How was her dad ever nervous?

"Yes, I was." Dad chuckled at himself. "I sat in the parking lot for fifteen minutes praying that I would have the strength to walk inside."

"Why were you nervous though?" Ashley sat up

now, too. "You're a great doctor, Dad."

"Thanks, Ash. But I didn't know back then if I'd be a great doctor. I had a lot to learn." He looked back at Kari. "All that to say, be confident. Have fun. It's okay to be nervous. But don't let it stop you from learning something new." He smiled. "Remember . . . the Bible says to be strong and courageous. Because God is with you wherever you go."

Kari yawned and laid back down on her pillow. "I like that." It was something their parents reminded them of often. God was with them. And He would be with her tomorrow.

Even if basketball PE day was the worst ever.

The sound of bouncing basketballs matched the pounding in Kari's heart.

I've played in the driveway lots of times, Kari kept reminding herself. But in a real gym, in front of her friends and teacher, Kari thought she'd rather do anything else.

Her mind went back to the conversation she'd had with her dad last night. God was with her wherever she went. *Yes, that's it,* she thought. *I'm not alone.*

Kari laced up her shoes. She watched some of the kids shooting hoops even before PE class began. They didn't need help or coaching, they already looked like pros after just a few days. She exhaled and turned her attention to the other shoe.

"Don't be nervous, Kari." Mandy sat down on the gym floor. "It's not even a big deal."

"Easy for you to say." Kari looked at her hands. They were shaking. "The ball might as well be square for as good as I dribble. You've seen me."

Mandy laughed. "You aren't that bad. Besides, even NBA players have to start somewhere."

"True." Kari pictured her dad the first time he went to the hospital as a doctor. Waiting in his car. Not wanting to do something embarrassing. Kari gathered up her courage. If her dad could be brave, so could she.

"Basketball!" Liza dribbled over to Kari. She bounced the ball in perfect rhythm without looking at it once. Then she dribbled between her legs and switched to the other hand. Kari's happy thoughts melted away.

Do not be afraid . . . God is with you.

There. Those words calmed Kari down.

"All right everybody." Their PE teacher, Mr Stone, blew his whistle. "Grab a basketball from the cart and line up on the baseline." His gruff voice got the students' attention right away. Kari wasn't sure where the baseline was. But she followed everyone else. It must have been the line under the hoop because that's where everyone gathered.

"We'll start with dribbling, then we'll play a game." The coach demonstrated like he'd done since last Thursday. *Bounce. Bounce. Bounce. Bounce.* "It's a rhythm. Keep the ball under your palm. Give it a try." He blew the whistle again and the students all began to dribble their basketballs.

Before she began, Kari watched her classmates around her. Some got it right away. Others struggled to keep the ball under their hands. Kari dribbled it a few times, but then the ball moved ahead of her and away from her hand. Kari ran after it and returned to the line.

Her heart was beating even harder than before.

"Just focus on feeling the ball under your hand, Kari." Liza's words were encouraging and helpful.

"Think of it like dancing. Just keep the beat."

Like dancing. Kari hadn't thought of it like that before. "Keep the beat. I can try that."

She tried again and a third time, and always the ball got away from her. But on the fourth time she actually could feel the beat. But then the ball hit her foot and spun out toward the middle of the court.

Mr. Stone picked up Kari's ball and bounced it back to her. "Keep working, Kari Baxter. You'll get it."

"Yes, sir." Kari grabbed the ball and exhaled. This was going to be harder than she thought. But as the class ended, Kari realized something.

She had survived another day of basketball. No one had laughed at her.

And she had never felt alone.

After school, Kari heard Luke playing basketball out in the driveway. At first that sound was the last thing Kari wanted to hear. But if anyone could help her, it would be her brother. Besides, she didn't want to hate PE every day for the rest of the unit. She wanted to get better and grow. And that required practice.

She took a drink of water and headed out to the basketball hoop. She watched her brother for a few minutes. Basketball was like breathing for Luke.

"Hey, Kari." Luke picked up the ball and tucked it under his arm. "Wanna play?"

"Actually, Luke . . ." Kari put her hands on her hips. "I'm in a tough situation."

Luke made another shot and then turned to her again. "What's up?"

"We're doing basketball in PE." Kari rambled. "And I can't get it."

Her younger brother smiled. "You came to the right guy."

"That's what I thought." Kari walked toward him. They started with dribbling.

"Dribbling is tricky." Luke demonstrated. "Well. It can be." He bounced the ball on the concrete. "You have to feel the ball under your hand." Luke tossed the basketball to Kari.

She really caught it. "Liza told me it was like dance. Just keep the beat."

"Sure." Luke nodded. "I can see that."

Kari began to dribble. One bounce at a time. And again, just like it had earlier in the day, the ball went away from her.

"I got it." Luke ran and got the ball this time. He bounced it back to Kari.

"Thanks." Kari shook her hands around, loosening up. "Here we go." After a few bounces Kari could feel herself improving, finding the rhythm. But then, once again, the ball bounced away from her. She grabbed it and huffed.

"It's okay, Kari." Luke smiled. "You have to bend your knees. Get low. It's no good if you stand straight and tall." Luke bent his knees, showing Kari the kind of stance she would need.

Kari took a deep breath and let it out. *Bend your knees,* she told herself. *Stay low.* Then she tried again. She wasn't sure if it was the practice or Luke's patience with her, but suddenly dribbling felt different.

She had found the beat.

Luke spoke over the sound of the bouncing ball. "Now slowly . . . walk toward me but keep dribbling."

Kari did just that. One step at a time. She focused on staying low, keeping the ball under her hand and going slowly.

"There you go, Kari!" Luke clapped and cheered for her.

She took three more steps, and she was still bouncing the ball next to Luke. "I did it!" She let the ball go and gave Luke a hug. "Thank you."

"You did great." Luke clapped. "See? It just takes practice."

"How'd you get so good at this? You're like . . . a professional." Kari was breathless. Gone were the nerves from earlier. Now, in this moment, her heart fluttered with joy.

"It's just natural." Luke picked the ball up and did some dribbling himself. He was much faster and smoother than Kari. "I mean, I'm out here practicing all the time. Before school. After school. But I love it. Like you love journaling. Or dancing." Luke shot the ball.

"Hmmm." Kari smiled. "For me, dribbling really is like a dance."

"Well, you're definitely getting it." Luke shot

the ball one more time, right into the net. "Pushing through is like a different kind of adventure. Cause you were willing to try something new. That's a key to any adventure."

"Thanks, Luke." Kari hugged him again and headed for the back door. "I have some writing to do."

"Glad I could help!" Luke waved at her.

Inside, Kari grabbed her journal from her backpack. She had to get this reminder down before she forgot.

She flopped on the couch and flipped to the page she had started a few days ago.

Kari Baxter's Reminders for Enjoying Any Adventure

Then she wrote a third reminder, the one she'd learned playing basketball today.

Expect the unexpected.
Try new things.
Confidence is key.

It was a rule she had learned from her dad, but also from a surprising tutor. Her younger brother, Luke, professional basketball star in training. She smiled at the new reminder.

Trying new things was essential because all adventures were new in some way.

Tomorrow basketball would be much different, Kari was sure. No more fear and trembling for her. Basketball dribbling was a dance with a beat all its own. And she would be better tomorrow than today.

Next time Kari took to the basketball court, she would be ready.

11

Setting Sail

ASHLEY

Monday afternoon homework was weighing on Ashley. She kept thinking about science camp. Earlier she had talked so much about that adventure that she had been sent to the living room to finish her math. Which was where she was now.

Living room math prison.

Ashley set her pencil down on her math book page and stared out the window across their big front yard. Bit by bit, a picture began to form. She and her friends digging up diamonds from a cave or gold from a stream. The group of them walking up the side of a volcano and running from hot lava minutes later. And of course, the bears.

The friendly wild bears.

Waiting for science camp was almost like waiting for Christmas.

Ashley looked around. Erin was reading across the room in the chair in the corner. Brooke and Kari were doing homework at the kitchen table. And the muffled sound of the basketball outside told them all that Luke was too young for any of this.

And Mom was at the grocery store getting food for the week. Dinner tonight? Leftover meatloaf.

Brooke flopped on the couch. "Finished. Finally." She sighed. "So much homework. This is the worst day!"

The worst day. Ashley thought about that. "Well . . . actually, it could be worse." She shut her math book and moved to the spot next to Brooke.

"How?" Brooke clutched a pillow.

"We could . . . be stranded in the desert. With no water. And a bunch of baby goats to look after. That would be worse." Ashley nodded. "Goats are not easy to take care of." At least, she imagined that was the case.

"I like goats." Erin kept her eyes on her book but added her thoughts anyway.

Brooke slumped forward on the pillow. "I want to go on a cruise."

"I agree." Erin set her book down. "I could read with the ocean wind in my face."

"I got it!" Ashley tapped Brooke's arm. "Let's do it. Let's go on a cruise!"

Brooke turned to her. "Ashley, you know we can't do that. Mom and Dad said."

"Yes, we can!" Ashley stood. "We can do a cruise right here! In the living room!" She could see it.

"Like . . . pretend?" A small smile made its way over Brooke's face.

"That's right, big sister." Ashley patted Brooke's shoulder. "You're never too old to pretend. Don't forget that."

Brooke set the pillow down and stood next to Ashley. "Okay. Show me."

"Come on!" Ashley ran into the kitchen to the cupboard with their art supplies. "We'll need paper. Lots of it."

Brooke helped her pull a box of paper from the cabinet. "How do we do this?"

"I'll show you." Ashley found the bin of colored pencils. "We'll make windows first."

"Can I join?" Erin shouted from the living room.

"Of course!" Brooke called back. "We need all hands on deck!"

Ashley moved to the kitchen table with the paper and pencils. "Brooke, get a pair of scissors and some tape!"

Kari joined them and the four sisters sat at the table, drawing and cutting out the oval shapes of the windows. Each window had some kind of ocean scene on it.

"Think beautiful," Ashley instructed her sisters. "Maybe a dolphin or birds on the horizon."

"I drew a mermaid." Erin pointed to her window.

Ashley gave her sister a thumbs-up. "Looks good."

The back door slid open and Luke stepped inside, breathless from playing basketball. He took one look at the art supplies on the table and rushed over. "What's going on?"

"We're making a living room cruise." Erin raised her eyebrows. "You should come with us, Luke!"

Ashley handed Luke two sheets of paper. "Here. Do two drawings just like what you'd see through a window on a cruise."

By the time they were all done, they had fourteen windows in total. Each person did two windows. But Ashley did four more, because she loved this living room cruise.

"Now." Ashley studied the windows. "We need to tape the windows to the walls."

Brooke took the tape and led everyone into the living room.

After the windows were all taped up, they surveyed their work. Ashley was impressed, but it didn't look much like a cruise ship. Not yet. "Hmmm." She tapped her chin.

"I know!" Luke jumped a few times. "It needs a captain's wheel!"

"Yes." Brooke squinted her eyes. "Where would we find that?"

"Hold on." Luke sprinted out of the room, and toward the garage.

"Marsha talked about the captain's dinner." Kari looked at her sisters. "We can definitely do that."

Brooke put her hands on her hips. "Carly told me that the ladies wore dresses and long white gloves. The men wore suits."

"It sounds like the best time." Ashley sighed.

Kari's eyes lit up. "Let's put on our best clothes and bring the kitchen chairs into the living room." The girls hurried and lined the chairs up, like seats on a cruise ship.

"We can use that folding table in the laundry room." Erin ran that direction. "Come help me, Brooke!" When the table was in place, they all took their seats.

"A living room captain's dinner!" Ashley squealed. "This is going to be really something."

Just then, Luke returned with an old bicycle wheel and a small garden shovel. He was wearing one of Dad's baseball caps. White and black. Like a captain's hat. "Here!" He placed the shovel against the bookcase, so the handle was sticking up, and he fastened the bike wheel to that. "Now we can steer this thing."

"Genius!" Ashley clapped. "Good job, Luke!"

"Nice hat!" Brooke saluted their little brother. "All right, Captain. Take us to the Bahamas!"

"Yes, ma'am!" Luke grabbed the wheel and pretended to steer. "Look! Dolphins up ahead on the left!"

The girls rushed to the left side of the room, giggling. They all peeked into the paper windows.

"I see them!" Erin tapped on the piece of paper. "There are so many!"

"Let's get ready for the captain's dinner." Brooke stepped away from the windows. "Everyone dress nice. I'll heat up the leftovers. And we'll meet back here."

"Love it!" Ashley sprang into action and ran upstairs with the others. She and Kari picked out cute dresses they had worn last Easter and rummaged through Mom's closet for sun hats. Also, they each slipped into a pair of her high heels. As they headed back downstairs, Ashley looked back at her sister.

"Dahhhling. You look absolutely mahhhvelous." Ashley used the same voice they used whenever they had a tea party with Mom.

Kari giggled. "Why thank you, dahhhling. You, as well."

In the living room, Brooke wore her long red Christmas dress. Also, she had set up the table in the living room cruise ship, with plates of their mother's leftovers.

Erin was dressed in a bathrobe. "It's a ball gown." She nodded.

The captain's hat was all Luke needed. He looked just exactly like a captain even in his gym shorts and T-shirt.

"Welcome to the captain's dinner!" Brooke announced. "Have a seat."

They ate their food and talked about the things they'd done on the island. Fishing and scuba diving with sharks and swimming with dolphins.

Eventually, Mom walked through the door with groceries and the cruise came to an end. Ashley and her siblings helped with the bags of food, and then Mom came on board the ship. After a short time at sea, their mother even helped clean up the paper windows.

That night before Ashley fell asleep, she thought about their living room cruise and how there would never be another one like it. Just so she'd never forget, she pulled out her sketch pad and drew herself and her brother and sisters sitting at the captain's dinner on a cruise to the Bahamas. Right in their own living room.

"Thank You, God, for siblings who are my best friends," she whispered as she finished the drawing. If Ashley had her way they'd never be bored again. Turning a homework day into the best day only took a little imagination.

And in this case, a whole lot of paper.

12

Checking Off the List

KARI

Between the lake hike and the living room cruise, Kari had almost forgotten about science camp. But the trip was Friday and today she had no choice but to think about it.

Because today they were shopping for camp supplies.

Kari looked out the window as they headed toward the store. She and Ashley were the only two kids with Mom on the shopping trip. Brooke was watching Erin and Luke at home and Dad would be back from work soon.

This time was for the science camp girls only.

In Mom's purse was a list of all the things Kari and Ashley would need for science camp. Mom was good at shopping for adventures like this.

They pulled into the parking lot and Kari read the sign. BLOOMINGTON SECONDS.

"Seconds?" Kari was in the front seat next to their mother. "Does that mean secondhand? I think new might be better."

"It does." Mom's tone was more cheerful than Kari's. "Everything doesn't have to be brand-new, Kari girl. Especially when we might only use it one time."

"That's good, Mother." Ashley nodded. "I like it. Smart shopping."

First off they headed for the shoe section. Mom pulled the list from her purse. "According to the list, you both need a pair of sturdy shoes or hiking boots." She looked over the wall of shoes. "There they are. Boots!" Mom handed Kari a pair. They had rough bottoms and thick laces. "These are your size."

Kari sat on the floor and slipped off her tennis shoes. She pushed her feet into the boots. The weight of them took her by surprise. She laced up the boots and stood.

"What do you think?" Mom crossed her arms, smiling.

Kari nodded. "They fit." She picked up her feet, one at a time. "But . . . they're kinda heavy."

Mom found a pair for Ashley, too. Ashley marched around like someone in the army. "I feel like a marina."

"Marine, Ashley." Kari giggled. "Marina is pizza sauce."

"Actually, that's marinara." Mom smiled. "Marina is a place where boats are parked."

Both girls agreed the boots would work, and once they'd put the boots in the cart they headed to another section of the store. They found flash-lights and overnight bags, and each girl got to pick out a baseball cap.

Finally, they each chose a jacket. Kari's was purple with yellow trim and a sturdy hood. Ashley's had rainbow stripes across the whole thing. And it also had a hood in case it rained.

"This is my coat of many colors, Mother!" Ashley did a little tap dance across the aisle. She finished it with a full circle twirl. "Science camp will be so much better in my coat of many colors. I'll be just like Joseph from the Bible!"

Mom grinned. "Only you would find a coat of many colors for science camp, Ashley." She nodded. "But I like your choices, girls. They're warm and waterproof."

At the checkout, they met a man named Walter. He had a long white beard and a bald head. They told him all about the science camp and how they were getting supplies.

"Mom said not everything has to be brand-new," Ashley told Walter.

"Your mom is smart." Walter smiled as he rang up Kari's heavy hiking boots.

"Do you like my coat of many colors? It's like Joseph. From the Bible story." Ashley was still wearing her coat. The sleeves were a little long, but Kari wasn't going to tell her that.

"I do like it." Walter seemed impressed. He had a kind face, which Kari liked.

Kari spotted a sign over the door that read: YOU'RE A BLESSING! "I like your sign." She looked at Walter. "Why does it say that?"

Walter glanced over at the sign and back at Kari. "Because every time you shop here, we donate money to people at the Bloomington Shelter. The money we bring in helps them get back on their feet."

"That's really nice of you." Kari put one of the bags in the cart.

"In fact, Bloomington Seconds helped me. I used to be in a sad place, but this secondhand store gave me a job and helped me figure out my life." Walter handed the last bag to Mom. "Have fun at science camp!"

Getting the items checked off the list made Kari a little more confident about science camp. She liked being prepared. And that wouldn't have happened without Mom's help. You could never have a good adventure without being ready. The list made sure you didn't forget something. And Mom never forgot anything.

She was always prepared.

As Kari climbed into her seat in the car it hit her. That was the next reminder on her Adventure list! She reached into the front seat pocket and pulled out her journal, flipping to the list. On line four she wrote out the next reminder:

> Kari Baxter's Reminders for Enjoying
> Any Adventure
>
> Expect the unexpected.
> Try new things.
> Confidence is key.
> Always be prepared.

Kari smiled at the list. Every reminder was important. And something else—they made her feel ready. She looked at her sturdy hiking boots in the bag beside her. Yes, for the first time, she was actually a little excited. In fact, she was more than excited.

Kari was prepared.

Now if she could just feel that way about basketball.

The next day while the basketball unit continued at school, Kari worked on her dribbling and passing. She was actually better than before.

Luke's help from the other day made a big difference. Chest pass, bounce pass, overhead pass. Dribbling around cones. She was no Michael Jordan by any means. But she *was* getting better. And that was making the unit at school more fun. The more confident Kari grew, the more fun she had.

Mr. Stone stood in front of Kari's PE class and checked the notes on his clipboard. "All right, class. Today we are going over dribbling and passing again."

"Yes," Kari whispered to Mandy and Liza. "Yes. That's exactly what I've been practicing." She examined the court. Cones had been set up at the free throw and half-court lines. The same way Luke did it.

Mr. Stone continued. "We will be dribbling around the first cone, then around the second, and then we'll make a straight line back to the baseline, where you will pass the ball to the next student in line. Use the pass of your choice." He walked to the ball cart. "Get in five lines." He tossed one basketball to each of the students at the front of the lines.

Three times in a row, Kari took the ball with

confidence. And she did exactly what Mr. Stone asked. She had done it! Because of her brother, Luke, Kari had conquered basketball!

On their break, Liza and Mandy sat with her on the gym floor. "My mom said it might be cold this week. At science camp." Liza pulled her hair back in a ponytail. "I hope you girls have good coats."

Kari nodded. "My mom just bought me one."

"Prepared. Nice." She gave Kari a high five.

Mandy tied her shoe. "My brother has been saying that science camp is where the teachers do science experiments on our brains." She rolled her eyes. "He's joking . . . I think."

"Experiments on our brains." Liza put her hands on her hips. "You can't believe something like that, Mandy."

"Well . . ." Mandy shrugged. "He's been before."

Kari refused to think about that. Of course, their teachers wouldn't do experiments on their brains. That was something Ashley would make up.

Even still, the possibility stayed with her.

As they walked through the school lobby, Kari noticed a table set up about science camp. She swallowed. Her confidence about that trip kept fading. Every time she wasn't actually thinking about it. The shopping trip had helped her wrap her head around what she would bring with her, which made her more prepared.

But she still had concerns.

At least she had tonight to be excited about. Tonight was her first dance class.

Good thing she didn't have Wednesday night church tonight.

But first Kari had to get through after school homework. When she finished with her math assignment, Luke went over some of his basketball pointers again.

"Now, remember . . ." Luke pushed back from the table, stood up, and bent his knees. "Keep yourself low. Athletic stance. Focus on the ball. Keep it under your hand."

"Got it." Kari ran through those things in her head.

"And keep your eyes up." Brooke cleaned the cookie crumbs off the kitchen counter. Cookies were their afternoon snack today. Always the best.

Brooke was still talking about her basketball skills. "I'm pretty good at it, myself. Don't let the ball hit your face." She laughed. "I learned that the hard way a few years ago." She rubbed her forehead, as if just bringing up the injury made it hurt all over again.

"Ouch." Erin frowned. "If it's that dangerous, I don't think I'll ever play."

"You have to." Ashley slurped down the last of her milk. "Everyone has to in PE. I'm already practicing for next year. I'm pretty good, if I don't say so."

Mom was in the kitchen getting napkins for the dinner table. "If you *do* say so, Ashley. You're pretty good if you *do* say so."

"Exactly." Ashley wiped her mouth. "That's what I said, Mother. If I don't say so myself."

Luke put his arm around Erin. "But don't worry, I'll teach you like I taught Kari."

"Yes, Luke is a very good coach." Kari couldn't finish her cookies fast enough. "And tomorrow we will see just how much you helped me, Luke."

Dinner flew by and suddenly it was time for

Kari's dance lesson. She grabbed her backpack and headed for the car. As she did, Kari said a little quiet prayer of gratitude in her heart. *God, thank You for my dance lesson tonight. Thank You for helping me be patient. And please, don't let a basketball hit my face like it hit Brooke's. Amen.*

On the way to her first dance lesson, Kari brought the science camp situation up to her mom. "You don't think the teachers experiment on our brains, right? At science camp?"

Mom glanced at her. "Absolutely not."

"Right." Kari laughed quietly at herself. "Mandy's brother. He has an imagination like Ashley's."

From the minute Kari walked into the dance studio, she felt like she was home. The parents sat in chairs at the back, so they could watch the lesson. And the students stood in front of the biggest mirror Kari had ever seen.

The dance teacher, Miss Lizzy, was one of the kindest people Kari had ever met. She said she learned to dance in Los Angeles and moved to Bloomington to study dance at Indiana University.

Miss Lizzy led them in warm-ups and stretches

and then it was time to do what she called technique.

"Okay, class. We will line up on one side of the room and do chassés across the floor. Like this." Miss Lizzy demonstrated. It was a sort of shuffle step with one foot in front and then the other. She led with her right foot. "One and two, change feet." She stepped forward with her left foot and continued. "Three and four." She turned and faced the class.

The move looked tricky, but Kari stayed confident.

"I know it's new for many of you . . ." Miss Lizzy pressed play on the sound system. Fun upbeat music blasted. "Just follow me," she shouted above the music. "It'll be great. Ready? Five . . . six . . . seven . . . eight . . ." The teacher chasséed across the floor.

Kari felt like a ballerina as she followed Miss Lizzy.

Next they did something called chaîné turns.

"It's pronounced sha-nay," Miss Lizzy explained. "Stay on your toes, and each time you turn, look at the sun sticker on the wall." She demonstrated, spinning like a ballet queen. When it was the class's turn, the movement made Kari a little dizzy. But she so enjoyed every moment. The class ended with stretching.

Finally, Miss Lizzy clapped. "Excellent job today, class. Give yourself a round of applause."

Everyone cheered and the girls headed back to their parents.

Kari ran to her mom. "How was that?"

Mom hugged her. "Oh, sweetheart." She clapped. "Beautiful job." Mom did a twirl. "I think I learned some of the moves." She gave it a try, chasséing toward the door.

Mom was actually pretty good at it.

After dinner, Kari taught her family some of the moves. Even Dad joined in.

"Okay. Let's see what I got." Dad followed Kari's lead on the chaîné turn.

"Make sure you stare at something on the wall, or you'll fall over," Kari encouraged him.

"Oh. I'm fine." Dad was confident. But a few spins in, he fell to his knees, too dizzy to keep going. The whole family gathered around him as their father spread out on the floor laughing. "I . . . am not cut out for dancing."

Everyone else started laughing, too, and all five kids helped Dad to his feet.

"I think if you had pointed your toes more." Ashley nodded. "Maybe next time."

They all laughed again. And when together they walked up the stairs that night, the giggling continued. "I think this makes us all best friends," Luke whispered to the girls.

"Definitely." Erin kept her voice soft. "The five Baxter best friends."

They all agreed and as Kari settled in for the night, she thought about Dad doing chaîné turns across the living room floor. She covered her mouth so her laugh wouldn't wake up Ashley. The mental image of her father's dance move made her think of something. One of the items already on her list of adventure reminders:

Confidence is key.

It was true. Just like Dad, if she believed she could, she would. Half of the battle of trying something new was putting one foot in front of the other and doing it. Like she had done with basketball. And even in the dance room. Maybe confidence was all Kari needed to make science camp a true success. She lay down on her pillow. Time would tell.

And she didn't have much of it left.

13

Same but Different

ASHLEY

As their car sped along the road, Ashley watched the lights whizzing by. It was like her own personal light show. *Zoom zoom zoom.* One after the other. She very much enjoyed it. They were headed to one of Dad's co-workers' houses for dinner.

"Dr. Pratik has children your age," Mom said as she looked over her shoulder at the five of them. "And they're serving traditional Indian food tonight." She didn't wait for a response. "You're going to love it!"

Brooke was sitting in the middle row near the passenger window. She leaned forward. "The Pratik family used to live in India, right?"

"They did." Mom nodded. "They have some very interesting stories to tell us."

Luke and Erin were in the backseat. Luke raised his hand. "I have a question."

"Yes, Luke?" Dad looked in the rearview mirror. His voice sounded like he knew what the question might be about.

"What if . . ." Luke paused. "What if we don't love the Indian food?"

"Yeah." Erin sounded concerned, but polite. "I don't love a lot of American foods. I've never even had Indian food."

Ashley nodded. "I must say, the youngest siblings do make a good point here, Parents." Ashley sat in the middle between Brooke and Kari. "About the food, that is."

Kari shrugged. "I say we at least try it. We might love it."

"That's the spirit." They were at a stoplight, so their father looked back at Kari and smiled. "Trying new foods is how you find some of your favorites. Favorites you didn't know you had!"

Ashley narrowed her eyes. That sounded

unlikely. Pizza and hamburgers were her favorites. Nothing they ate tonight would probably change that. Still, she was glad the Pratik family had a girl her age. Maybe they could make a comic book together.

About cooking new food!

"When did the Pratik family live in India?" Brooke put her hand on their mother's seat. "I can't wait to hear about that."

"They lived there two years ago." Mom smiled at Dad. "I'll let the Pratiks tell you about it."

"So, are we going to India?" Luke shouted from the back. "Cause . . . I didn't pack a bag." He sounded sort of panicked.

Mom laughed. "No. We're going to Martinsville." She looked out the window at the houses they were passing. "Remember. It's Dr. and Mrs. Pratik."

"Nice, honey." Dad glanced at Mom.

In Mom's other hand was a bouquet of flowers that she had brought as a gift. Ashley liked that about Mom. She always thought of everything. And she especially always thought of others. Dad pulled up in front of a house and parked the car. Once they were all outside, Dad led the way toward the house.

Ashley followed the family up the walkway that led to the Pratik family's front door. It was a spectacular brick home. Beautiful plants and trees out front were lit up by lights like the shops in downtown Bloomington. There was a fountain near the front door. And two big Beauty and the Beast lamps on either side of the double glass doors. Beauty and the Beast because last time Ashley saw lights like that was in that movie.

"This looks like a castle." Ashley stared at Kari. "A cozy castle."

Mom held the flowers as they reached the door. "Don't forget to use your inside voices." She turned and looked at each of them. "Let's respect their home." Mom focused on Ashley. "And don't be wild."

Ashley put her hand on her chest. "Me?"

"Yes." Dad smiled at her. "Remember the ice cream social?"

For a few seconds Ashley remembered. At the

school's welcome back event, she had slipped on the gym floor, and in a panic, threw her bowl of ice cream in the air. It landed on her teacher's head. "Okay." She nodded. "Not my proudest moment. I won't be wild tonight."

"Thank you." Mom pushed the doorbell. "It'll be a great night."

"Most of all, let's remember to be kind." Dad gave the kids a thumbs-up. "That's what sets us Baxters apart."

Dad knocked on the door and a few seconds later it opened and a man stood in the doorway. He had a big smile on his face.

"John." He shook Dad's hand.

Dad smiled. "Aryan. This is my family. Elizabeth, my wife. And my kids, Brooke, Kari, Ashley, Luke, and Erin."

"Hello, family! What a beautiful group. Welcome to our home." Dr. Pratik stepped back. "Please, join us."

Ashley tried not to stare, but inside the house was even more beautiful. A shimmering chandelier hung from the ceiling and beautiful paintings decorated the walls. The kind of paintings she was going to do when she was older.

The smell coming from the kitchen was different. But it was a good kind of different. They followed Dr. Pratik to where Mrs. Pratik was cooking dinner. She removed a dish from the oven.

"My love, look!" Dr. Pratik motioned to Ashley and her family. "The Baxters are here!"

Mrs. Pratik dried her hands on an apron and walked up, shaking hands with each of the kids and giving Mom and Dad each a hug. "We've been looking forward to this."

Mom handed over the flowers. "Thank you for having us."

The doctor's wife put the flowers in a vase and smiled at each of them. "I hope you're hungry!"

A dark-haired girl bounced into the kitchen. She walked up to Ashley and Kari. "Hi! I'm Meena. I'm in fifth grade."

Ashley gasped. "Same with me! I'm in fifth grade, too!"

Mrs. Pratik motioned for them to follow her to the dining room. There on the table was a spread of dishes Ashley didn't recognize. She felt her eyes get wide, but she calmed them down.

Wide eyes over this food could be rude. She checked with her siblings and they all seemed to be trying to keep their eyes normal. Like they weren't surprised about the things on the table.

"Why don't you tell us what you've cooked tonight?" Dr. Pratik put his arm around his wife's shoulder. "You've been working all day, dear."

"I started yesterday." Mrs. Pratik pointed to a plate of bread-like circles. "These are masala dosas. Sort of like an Indian pancake."

"What's it made of?" Luke peered over the edge of the chair. "It doesn't smell like a pancake."

Dr. Pratik laughed. "Oh, it's different, for sure, my boy. But it's very good."

Ashley stared at Luke. Dad was doing the same thing. "Let's let Mrs. Pratik explain her cooking." His tone said no one should ask questions until the pretty woman was finished talking. Ashley bit her tongue just a little, so she would remember.

Mrs. Pratik moved the plate of masala dosas closer. "I made the batter yesterday. It has to soak at least twenty-four hours. It's made of rice, flour, and lentils."

"Hmm." Ashley nodded. "Very nice." She smiled at her father. "Very, very nice."

"Yes, and over here . . ." Mrs. Pratik moved down the table to the next dish. "This is an appetizer. We call it chaat. It's a savory snack. It's made of potato pieces, crispy fried bread, and chickpeas. And the sauce is yogurt, ginger, and tamarind sauce."

The Baxter children were speechless.

"You've worked so hard on this, Raju," Mom said. Mom could use Mrs. Pratik's first name. "We're honored."

Mrs. Pratik's smile was easy. Like she expected the Baxter kids to be a little startled at this menu. She looked straight at Ashley. "Do you know what chaat means?"

"It means . . . a good conversation?" Ashley tried to connect that to food. "Snacks for a good conversation maybe?"

"Nice try." Dr. Pratik chuckled. "It means finger-licking. So good you want to get every drop."

Ashley nodded. Her siblings did the same thing.

Spread out over the table were jars of different sauces and spreads. None of them looked familiar.

Mrs. Pratik finished explaining the food. Their main course was chicken makhani, which looked like spaghetti sauce with chicken pieces. "It's also called butter chicken. We'll serve it over red lentils. Then for dessert we'll have traditional barfi."

"Yes, barfi is typically served at weddings, but we wanted to do something special for tonight."

Barfi. Ashley let the word mull around in her mouth. She could feel her father watching her. Her mom, too. Slowly, Ashley nodded. "I've always wanted to try . . . barfi."

There was a moment, and then everyone laughed. "I promise you"—Dr. Pratik patted Ashley's head— "it tastes better than it sounds."

Once they were all seated, Dr. Pratik prayed. "Lord, thank You for bringing our families together to celebrate our love for You and for each other. You are a good God. In Jesus's name, amen."

"Amen." Ashley joined her voice with the others. Prayer was something they had in common. She looked at the display of food. Where to start?

she wondered. Probably not with the barfi.

As it turned out, Mrs. Pratik served the plates, starting each of them out with small amounts of the food.

"Do you eat this way every night?" Luke looked at the doctor and his wife. "Seems like a lot of work."

"It is." Mrs. Pratik grinned at Luke. "And no, we don't."

"Definitely not." Meena giggled. "We usually eat spaghetti or meatloaf."

"Or pizza!" Her little brother, Alan, raised his fork. "Pizza is my favorite."

"I love hamburgers." Dr. Pratik smiled at his wife. "This is indeed a special occasion."

Ashley tapped her fork around the butter chicken. It didn't smell as strange as it looked. She took a bite and suddenly her whole mouth had a little party. "Mrs. Pratik! This chicken is amazing!"

The same was true for the Indian pancakes and the little savory snacks and the chopped lentils. It was all good! "Mom, maybe you can get the recipes for this great stuff." Ashley waved her fork over the food on her plate. "Especially these pancakes."

Finally, it was time for the barfi. Ashley planned to just politely pass. *Barfi* was . . . well, it wasn't her best word. Mrs. Pratik put a piece on each of their plates. Ashley caught a smell of it. Sort of a milky smell. She was about to push back from the table, but just then Luke took a bite. Then Brooke and Kari and Erin. And their parents. And Meena and her brother.

And the whole room was talking all at once. "This is the best dessert I've ever had!" Luke held up his piece. "Can I have seconds, please, Mrs. Pratik?"

Kari said the same thing. Brooke looked at their mother. "You need the recipe for this, too."

Fine, Ashley told herself. She took a bite of her barfi square and . . . Ashley stood straight up. "What in the world?" At the same time, she caught Brooke's shocked look. Ashley dropped right back to her chair. "Barfi is . . . it's super-extra-delicious! I expected it to taste like—"

"Ashley." Her dad looked at her. "That's enough."

Ashley put her hand over her mouth. Her father

was right. She had almost said much more than she meant to say. She chewed the barfi and swallowed it. Then she took another bite and another. And two more pieces. "Brownies only wish they were barfi squares, Mrs. Pratik."

Everyone laughed. Because probably everyone knew what Ashley had almost said. Ashley thought if she could have a talk with the inventor of the barfi name, she would make a suggestion. Maybe call it something else.

When they were done with the excellent food, Meena hopped off her chair. "Hey, girls . . . want to see my room?"

"Yeah, and, Luke, you can come see my Lego collection. I have three full bins," Alan motioned to their brother.

"Really?" Luke raced after Meena's little brother.

The girls followed Meena. In her room was the most magical thing Ashley had ever seen. Her bed was built a few stairs up off the floor in the corner of the room. And all around it hung sheer pink curtains.

Her bedroom looked like a palace!

But that wasn't what Meena wanted to show them. She brought out something that surprised Ashley even more.

A sketchbook. "I love drawing." She looked at each of them. "Do any of you like art?"

"Like it?" Ashley raised both arms. "Art is my life!"

Meena clapped. "Then we're the same, you and me!"

"Yes, we are." Ashley took hold of Meena's hands and they danced around in a circle for a long moment. "I found another artist . . . I found another artist . . ." Ashley sang. She made up the tune as she went along.

Brooke and Kari and Erin sat cross-legged on the floor and watched.

After a minute, Ashley ran out of lyrics for that song. She stopped and put her hands on her knees so she could catch her breath. "I can't believe . . . I found my twin!"

Meena laughed. "I always wanted a twin." Meena opened her sketchbook and showed Ashley and her sisters several of her best drawings.

Ashley gasped when Meena showed them a sketch of a giraffe. "I drew that exact same thing when my class went to the zoo!"

Pride came over Meena's face. "I think the giraffe drawing is my best one."

After Meena put the sketchbook down, Brooke pointed to a photo album. "What's that?"

"That?" Meena looked over. "Pictures from when we lived in India." She pulled the album from the bookcase. "I'll show you."

For the next ten minutes Meena went through the photographs of her past. She handed the collection to Brooke. "You can look through the rest if you want."

"Do you miss living in India?" Brooke turned the pages of the photo album, studying the buildings and faces of kids that were Meena's old friends.

Meena's smile looked sad now. "Yes. I still miss it."

"I understand." Ashley dropped to the floor next to Brooke. "We moved here from Michigan. Getting used to Indiana took time."

"How did you do it?" Meena took a pillow from the floor and hugged it close.

Ashley thought about this. "I'm not a professional. I just learned to trust God. That eventually this place would feel like home."

"I did the same thing." Kari nodded, and Brooke and Erin did as well. "We're all getting used to Indiana."

"Yes!" Meena's face lit up. "Mom and Dad say to trust God, too. We have had to do that a lot since leaving India." "Why would you ever leave such a cool place as India! Sounds like the most adventurous beautiful place to live." Ashley thought India sounded cooler than Indiana. Even though, now that she thought about it, they sounded similar. Maybe whoever discovered Indiana was from India.

"Well . . . we didn't have a choice. There was a lot of danger in India, especially since we were Christians. My parents wanted us to grow up in a safe environment. So, we left everything." Meena shook her head, her eyes wide, as if remembering it was still just as hard.

Ashley couldn't imagine having to leave home because you weren't safe.

"That must have been so scary."

"It was. But Daddy said to treat it like an adventure." She opened her arms wide. "A very big adventure. And it has been nothing but that. I still feel like I am learning English."

"Your English is better than mine. I get words mixed up," Ashley confessed.

Meena sighed. "I wish you girls were at my school. Not everyone is as nice as you."

Ashley had personal experience with that truth. She patted Meena's hand. "There will always be mean people. My dad says it's because something is wrong with them."

"Yes." Brooke joined in. "Hurt people hurt people. That means when someone is hurting on the inside, they are sometimes mean enough to hurt someone else."

"For me"—Ashley grinned—"if someone is mean, I just beat them in a race. Like this mean boy Chris that I beat. That quieted him down." Ashley stuck her chin in the air.

"I like that." Meena laughed.

All of a sudden Ashley remembered something.

"Guess what, Meena? We're going to science camp tomorrow!" Ashley stood and did a victory lap around Meena's bedroom. Then she sat back down with the other girls. "Actual science camp!"

"No way!" Meena gasped. "I'm going with my school next week." Meena stood and did a victory lap of her own. When she sat down again they were all laughing.

"You really did find your twin, Ashley." Kari clapped. "You two are hilarious."

A few minutes later, Dad came looking for them. "Time to go, girls! Tomorrow's a big day for Kari and Ashley."

Kari looked a little sick at the idea. Ashley put her arm around her sister's shoulder. "Don't worry. I'll stick by your side when we visit the volcano."

They all laughed again. Which was strange to Ashley. Because what was so funny about a volcano?

As they were saying their goodbyes, Meena gave Ashley a hug. "Have fun at science camp. You'll have to tell me all about it next time we're together."

"You know something, Meena." Ashley put her

hand on her new friend's shoulder. "I think we're kindred spirits."

"I think so, too! Have fun!" She waved at Ashley and Kari and the others as they headed for the car.

On the way home, Ashley's mind went from one adventure to the next. She had to pack. Because the bus for science camp was leaving in the morning.

And she didn't want to forget anything.

Back at the house and before packing, Ashley did a quick sketch of herself with Meena, both girls painting at separate easels. Twin friends with everything in common.

Ashley closed her sketchbook and found the science camp packing list on her dresser. Across the

room, Kari was doing the same thing.

"Jeans. Check." Ashley grabbed two pair and tossed them in her bag. "Raincoat. Check." On top of the jeans, she folded her raincoat of many colors.

Brooke and Erin entered their room. "We'll miss you." Erin walked up to Ashley. "Friday to Monday seems like a long time."

"I still don't want to go." Kari finished packing and jumped up on her bed.

Ashley was looking for the best shoes to wear on the bus tomorrow. But also for hiking up a volcano. "Hey, Brooke." Ashley stuck her head out of the closet. "What kind of shoes do I need for an actual volcano?"

Brooke smiled. "You won't see a real volcano, Ashley. But if you do . . . your boots you got the other night should work just fine. Something to keep the lava away."

Ashley yelled from inside the closet. "If there really ends up being no volcano . . ." She grunted as she sifted through her clothes and shoes. "Then maybe we'll pan for actual gold in the stream. Or find dinosaur remains on the hillside. We might visit a worm farm and meet a real-life family of worms."

Then she spotted them. The most perfect pair of shoes for tomorrow. Her ballet slippers from playing Wendy at the talent show! She grabbed them and walked them to her bag on top of her bed. "The finishing touch." Ashley placed the slippers in the bag, beaming with pride.

"You're not supposed to pack those." Kari sounded nervous. "Mom said."

Ashley faced her sister. "I'm not packing them. I'm wearing them. On the bus."

"Okay." Kari shrugged. "Whatever you think."

Ashley turned back to the beautiful Wendy ballet slippers. They were perfect for the bus ride to science camp.

Because science camp was going to be an adventure as great as Neverland.

14

Cabins and Clown Shoes

ASHLEY

The next morning, no one noticed Ashley was wearing her Wendy ballet slippers. Not Mom as they left for school and not Mr. Garrett as she boarded the bus for science camp. Her jeans had a fun flare to them, which did a good job of hiding her shoes.

They were for sure the right shoes for the bus ride. Magical and full of wonder. Plus, she'd switch to her sturdy boots once she got to science camp.

Halfway to camp the bus ride started getting bumpy. Very bumpy.

Ashley sat next to Natalie, and Elliot and Landon were in the seat across the aisle. In front of Ashley were Kari and Mandy and Liza.

For science camp, the fifth and sixth graders would be mixed together. Already the teachers had assigned groups. Ashley's group included Kari and Mandy and Liza, and Natalie, Landon, Chris, and Elliot. They sat near the back, but they were the best eight students on the bus, probably.

At least Ashley thought so

Mr. Garrett was their personal chaperone. Which meant Ashley would have to be on her best behavior. That's what Dad had said last night. "Be on your best behavior, Ashley."

He didn't have to remind Kari.

Elliot and Landon were on their fifth bus sing-along song. "The . . . wheels on the bus go shwo-shwo-shwo, all through the tooooowwwwwwn!" Elliot's voice rang out louder than Landon's.

No one else was singing with them, so it was more like a duet.

"Elliot." Natalie leaned around Ashley. "It's round and round," Natalie corrected him. "Not shwo-shwo-shwo."

Elliot frowned. "No. I'm pretty sure it's shwo-shwo-shwo."

Ashley slumped in her seat. "All I know is the wheels on this bus better go fast-fast-fast. All these bumps are making me nervous. What if we break down and get eaten by a pack of wolves?"

Kari popped up from in front of Ashley and smiled at Elliot and Landon. "My sister is a little dramatic."

"We know." Elliot and Landon and Natalie answered all at the same time."

"I'm not dramatic." Ashley tucked her Wendy ballet slippers beneath her seat so no one would see them. "I'm . . . effervescent. That's all."

Just then the bus went over an extra-big bump and the kids all flew up in their seats. Some of them laughed and others held on to the seats in front of them.

"What is happening?" Ashley grabbed Natalie's arm with one hand, and the seat with the other. "This thing is out of control. Plus . . . no seatbelts."

Ashley looked toward the front of the bus. What if it went flying off the edge of the road? The wheels might fly off, even. And what if it went faster and faster until it began to fly? Or what if it broke down in the middle of the highway?

Then they'd never get to science camp.

The bus hit another big bump and again the kids bounced high in their seats. Ashley stood up. "We're breaking down!" Her announcement caught the attention of kids from four rows in either direction. They all cast nervous looks in her direction.

"Why would we break down?" Landon leaned past Elliot and stared at Ashley. "We're going along just fine."

"Yeah." Elliot grinned. "The wheels on the bus are still moving."

Ashley was still standing. "That can happen, just so you know. Bumps can make a bus break down. One too many bumps and—" She spread her hands out in front of her like an umpire calling "safe" at home plate. "Kerplat! The bus falls apart. Right in the middle of the road!"

Landon shook his head. "Ashley, you're making that up."

"I am not." Ashley bit her lip. It was time to talk to their teacher. He would know what to do. She scooted around Natalie into the aisle of the bus and took careful steps to the front, where the chaperones and teachers sat.

She tapped her teacher's shoulder. "Excuse me. Mr. Garrett?"

"Ashley." He spun around, clearly confused. "What are you doing? You're supposed to stay in your seat."

"Yes." She drummed her fingers on Mr. Garrett's seat top. "The problem is . . . some of us are worried about those last few big bumps. It feels like we may break down."

Mr. Garrett raised his eyebrows. "We are not going to break down. I'm sure about that."

Ashley looked out the window, at the trees whizzing by. "Okay. But those were two very rough bumps. You have to agree about that."

"They were. That happens. Especially with buses." He reassured her. "Don't worry. We are very safe. Please get back to your seat."

Ashley studied him. "Okay. If you say so." She took a few steps back to her seat, then she turned around and stood next to Mr. Garrett again. "You're sure?"

Her teacher sighed. "Yes, Ashley. I'm sure. Please sit down."

"Okay." She hesitated, but she'd said all she could say. The students were all watching her, but Ashley didn't care. She had spoken on behalf of the people, and now she returned to her seat proudly. Head in the air.

She slid past Natalie and took her seat next to the window.

"Well?" Elliot's eyes were wild with anticipation. "Are we gonna break down?"

"The answer is—" Ashley tried to believe the information herself. "We are not going to break down. At least Mr. Garrett doesn't think we will."

Elliot took a deep breath and began to sing once more. "Ninety-nine bottles of milk in the fridge, ninety-nine bottles of milk. Take one out, pass it about, ninety-eight bottles of milk in the fridge." He waved his hands over his head. "Come on, people! Everyone this time!"

"Yeah, everyone!" Landon waved his hands, too.

A few of the students joined in on the song, and then a few more, until practically all the kids on the bus were singing. Ashley was impressed. Elliot and Landon definitely had a leadership way about them.

Which just might come in handy once they finally reached science camp.

After four more near breakdowns and lots more bumps, the bus finally pulled up at science camp and parked. They hadn't broken down, after all! Single file they all walked off the bus and followed their leaders to the cabins. Boys' cabins were on one side of the camp, girls' on the other.

When she reached her cabin, Ashley ran inside. Kari was right behind her. "We're here! We made it!" Ashley did a few twirls across the wood floor. "See, Kari? I can do the chaîné turn, too."

Kari and her friends all did the same spinny turns, and the other girls filed in behind them. Each of them did the dance turn, too. "We are the dancing cabin, apparently," Ashley called out.

Kari's teacher, Ms. Nan, was in their cabin, along with a few moms who had come along to help. The cabin had a very distinct smell. It was like campfire and wood and memories, all mixed together.

Ten bunk beds lined the walls and a name of a student was taped to the foot of each bed. Ashley found her bed—a lower bunk—and she tossed her bag on the mattress. "Kari, look! You're on the top bunk!"

Kari walked over to the bunks and sighed. "Well, we're here."

"Is that . . . a smile I see?" Ashley's jaw dropped.

"Maybe." Kari couldn't hide it, a full-blown smile crept across her face. "Okay. I have to admit. This is pretty cool. And the walk up here was beautiful."

"So many pretty trees. And I saw a deer!" Ashley hugged Kari. "I *knew* this was going to be the best trip."

"Okay, girls!" Ms. Nan held up one hand. "Listen up. Please change into your sturdiest shoes or boots—if you haven't already done that. We'll head to the cafeteria for lunch in ten minutes. Welcome to science camp!" Her announcement was met with cheers and then everyone began changing their shoes.

Ashley unzipped her bag and began taking things out. Her boots should've been on top.

"I can't believe you wore your Wendy slippers to science camp." Kari stepped back and stared at Ashley's feet. "How did Mom let you out of the house like that?"

"Distraction?" Ashley kept searching through her bag.

"Mr. Garrett didn't notice, either?" Mandy walked up. "Good thing you brought the right shoes in your bag."

"Yep." Ashley's heart began beating very fast inside her chest. "I definitely did bring them. I know I did." She grabbed a pair of socks and threw them on the mattress. Next her raincoat of many colors and then her jeans. One item after another until . . .

Nothing. There was absolutely nothing at all left in the bag.

"Ashley!" Kari gasped. "You didn't bring your boots?"

"I did." Ashley fell to the edge of her bunk mattress and stared into her empty bag. "I remember putting them on top." She looked up at the ceiling. "There must've been a boot thief on that bus."

"No." Kari shook her head. "I saw you take the boots out last night. Before we fell asleep."

Ashley thought about that terrible news. Why would she do such a thing? Her brain remembered last night and then it hit her. "I did take them out! Because I thought I would wear them on the bus." She turned to Kari. "But then I decided the Wendy slippers would be better for the bus ride and . . ."

"You forgot to put your boots back in the bag." Mandy put her hands on either side of her face. "Ashley! You mean you have only your Wendy slippers for three days at science camp?"

Liza joined them then. "Are you kidding?" She stared at Ashley's slippered feet. "You don't have any other shoes but *those*?"

Kari and her friends stood there, all in a row, frozen in shock. Ashley tried to picture walking up the side of a volcano or panning for gold in her satin Wendy shoes. Tears stung at the corners of her eyes and she couldn't get a full breath.

Ms. Nan must've realized something was wrong

because she walked over to the girls. Kari explained the situation. "Ashley . . ." Ms. Nan sat beside Ashley on her bunk. "You don't have any other shoes? Not even tennis shoes? Nothing?"

"No." Ashley sniffed. "I'm sh- sh- shoeless."

"We'll figure something out." Ms. Nan stood and looked around. By now all the other girls had left for the cafeteria. Liza and Mandy joined them, but they both promised to look for leftover shoes. "In case someone left a pair in the cafeteria." Mandy waved. "See you at lunch."

"Hang on. I have an idea." Ms. Nan ran to the cabin door.

"Ms. Nan!" Ashley called after her. "Where are you going?"

Kari's teacher didn't stop. "I'll be right back!"

Natalie came running in. "Ashley! I heard what happened!"

"Yes." Ashley pinched her nose so she wouldn't cry. She pointed to her ballet slippers. "I . . . I made a big mistake."

"You didn't bring any shoes? Or boots? For the whole weekend?" Natalie covered her mouth for a

202

few seconds. A nervous laugh escaped through her fingers. "Oh, Ashley. That's terrible."

"Don't laugh!" Ashley crossed her arms. "You're supposed to be my best friend."

"I'm not laughing." Kari patted Ashley's shoulder.

Natalie seemed more in control of herself. "I'm sorry, Ashley. It's just . . . that could only happen to you."

Ashley thought about that. "You have a point."

Ms. Nan burst through the door again, breathless. "Here! I found these." She held out two plastic grocery bags. "You can wear them over your slippers. At least you'll stay dry."

"Ms. Nan." Ashley wanted to stay polite. "I don't think that will help. If I'm honest."

The teacher dropped down to the floor and attached one bag at a time to Ashley's slipper feet. "It's better than nothing."

Natalie and Kari stood back, side by side. Their eyes were wide, and their mouths hung open. Like this time . . . there really were no words. "Wow," Kari said.

Ashley stood and kicked one foot forward, then

the other. The bags puffed out with each kick.

Ms. Nan put her hands on her hips. "I like it, Ashley. That'll work just fine."

All three girls turned to Ms. Nan. Natalie spoke first. "She . . . she looks like a . . . clown." Natalie said the word as soft as she could. Then she winced. "Don't you think, Ms. Nan?"

"Definitely not." Ms. Nan rubbed her hands on her jeans. "Lots of people wear plastic bags over their shoes. To keep them clean and dry."

"I don't just look like a clown." Ashley blew her hair from her face. "I actually *am* a clown." She raised her hands and dropped them again. "I wore Wendy slippers to science camp."

That comment made Natalie and Kari both laugh. Quiet at first but then louder. Even after they covered their mouths with their hands, their laughter grew. And finally, that made Ashley and even Ms. Nan laugh.

"Come on, girls." Ms. Nan led the way to the door again. "Let's go to lunch."

Kari and Natalie walked on either side of Ashley. "Thank you." Ashley kept her head low. "Maybe the other kids won't notice my bag feet."

Ms. Nan went to sit with the other teachers and the parents. And Ashley, Kari, and Natalie grabbed sack lunches and sat next to Elliot and Liza and Mandy. Also at the table were Landon and Chris and a few other classmates.

"Hello, friends!" Ashley shouted as she sat down. She waved her hands and smiled big. Anything to take attention off her plastic bag shoes. She kept her voice louder than usual. "So, how's the lunch?"

"Why are you talking like that?" Elliot gave Ashley a side eye. "Are you nervous or something?"

"No!" Ashley laughed. "Why would I be nervous? I am calm. And cool. I'm normal. And excited. This is going to be another bonanza, Elliot. Plus, I have everything I need. I have shoes."

There was a brief moment of silence. Then . . . "Ashley forgot her shoes!" Natalie blurted out the announcement. "She has bags on her feet."

Ashley dug her elbow into her friend's side, but not too hard. "Natalie!"

"What? It's true." Natalie shrugged. "They're going to notice it sooner or later."

Chris laughed. "Ashley. Of course, that would happen to *you*."

"Really, Ashley?" Landon put his sandwich down on his bag. "You have no shoes at all?"

"No." Ashley shook her head. "No, that's not exactly true, Landon." Ashley kicked one foot up in the air and held it there. "I have my Wendy slippers. If Wendy were here right this minute, she would tell you . . ." She looked at the others. "She would tell *all* of you that Wendy slippers are perfectly fine shoes."

"Just not for . . . science camp." Landon was the only one not laughing.

Mr. Garrett walked up to their table. "How's my group doing?" He had a clipboard and made notes. Probably about who was here.

"Yeah. We're great." Ashley smiled wide. "No issues here."

Mr. Garrett touched the pen to his lips and squinted. "Are you sure? Something seems . . . off." He glanced down at Ashley's feet. "What are those?"

Ashley looked down at her feet. "Oh! You mean,

my plastic bag shoes? It's a fashion trend. From . . . Paris."

"Ashley. Did you forget your shoes?" Mr. Garrett stared at her. He looked like he might faint from the shock.

A long sigh came from Ashley. "Yes, Mr. Garrett. I did, in fact, forget my shoes. Boots, to be exact."

Landon was on his feet. "Hey, Mr. Garrett. I have an extra pair." Landon ran out of the lunchroom. When he returned he held up a pair of sneakers. "You can use these, Ashley."

She remembered to smile. The shoes were large and dirty white. But they were better than plastic bags. "Thank you, Landon. I will . . . treasure your shoes during science camp."

Landon grinned at that.

"Perfect." Mr. Garrett took a step back. "Looks like we're off to a great start."

When he was gone, Ashley removed the plastic bags from her feet and slipped Landon's old tennis shoes over her Wendy slippers. But when she stood and tried to take a step, Landon's shoes slipped right off.

"Use the plastic bags." Kari pointed to the crumpled bags on the floor. "Stuff them in around your toes."

The day kept getting more humiliating. Ashley dropped to the floor and packed the toes of Landon's shoes with the plastic bags. This time when she stood, the shoes stayed on. Later, she'd have to draw a picture of herself in these things. Though she still couldn't see climbing a volcano with them.

"All right, students." Mr. Garrett was at the front of the cafeteria now. "Clean up your trash and let's meet outside for the first experiment."

The fifth and sixth graders did as they were asked. Ashley was slower than the others because every step was more of a shuffle. Like she was ice skating.

"Clown feet." Chris whispered the words as she walked past. "Ashley Baxter has clown feet!"

"Chris." Ms. Nan was standing nearby. "I heard that. You will go back to the cafeteria and help wash water cups."

"What?" Chris looked shocked. "I was just having a little fun."

"Yes." Ms. Nan motioned to one of the parent volunteers. "Now you'll have a little fun washing dishes."

Ashley felt her eyes grow wide. She looked at Natalie and then Kari. All of them kept their eyeballs to themselves. At the same time the parent took Chris to the cafeteria. Ashley leaned close to Kari. "I like your teacher."

"She's the best." Kari gave Ashley a thumbs-up.

The first experiment was not hiking up a volcano or making friends with wild bears. It wasn't even panning for gold.

It was gathering ten different types of leaves. Ashley shuffled about with her group until they had a bag full of leaves. Like they could get any old day in the Baxters' backyard. They roasted marshmallows around the fire that night and then Ashley tramped her way up the hill with Kari and Mandy and Liza.

Maybe tomorrow would be more adventurous.

As she took off Landon's shoes, she did her own little laugh. Because those things looked ridiculous.

"Hey, Kari," Ashley whispered when the cabin

lights were out. "Do you think Mom and Dad would give me clown lessons?"

"No." Kari's giggle pierced the night air. "Go to sleep, Ashley."

"Okay." Ashley laughed to herself.

She had to admit it: Chris was right. In Landon's sneakers, Ashley really did look like a clown. She even walked like one.

Now if only she could talk her parents into clown lessons.

15

An Actual Volcano

KARI

They were not going to make friends with wild bears today. But Kari did wonder if they might see bears. Especially that morning when their groups all set out for the woods. By themselves. Without any other groups in sight.

At least Mr. Garrett was with them. Kari studied the man walking at the head of the group. *He could take on a bear, right?* she asked herself. All of a sudden Mr. Garrett didn't look as tall as before. Kari kept her focus on the nature around them.

Best not to think about the bears.

Shuffling along beside her was Ashley in Landon's tennis shoes, her friend Natalie, and

Mandy and Liza. The boys were walking up ahead a little way with the teacher.

"Okay." Kari read from the worksheet. "According to this, we have to go to the creek and collect water samples using our beakers." She tapped one of the plastic tubes they had been given.

"Why is it called a beaker?" Ashley pulled the plastic tube from her backpack and held it close to her face. "Maybe . . . it's a bird feeder."

"Close." Elliot dropped back so he was shoulder to shoulder with Ashley and Kari. "But it's actually called a beaker because the tops of the tubes have little spouts that *look* like bird beaks. See?" Elliot tapped the edge of the item. "Also something about the Beaker people a long time ago. That's what my dad told me."

"I'm impressed." Kari raised her eyebrows. "You continue to surprise me, Elliot."

The ground was hillier now. Straight up. A couple times Ashley fell forward when her long shoes got stuck in leaves or tree roots. Then, without warning, the ground began to rumble.

Ashley stopped. "Take cover!"

"What?" Kari ducked. "Ashley! What did you see?"

"Yeah, what's happening?" Natalie stood behind Kari.

Mandy and Liza bunched together, too. Liza gazed to the right and then the left. "Is it an earthquake?"

Ashley pointed up ahead. "Stop!" She shuffled fast ahead of the other girls to Mr. Garrett and the boys. "Take cover, I say! Everyone! Quick."

The rumbling was growing louder.

Mr. Garrett and the boys turned and faced Ashley. The teacher took a step toward her. "What is it, Ashley?"

"Don't you feel that?" Ashley spread her arms. "We found it!"

"What?" Elliot pushed his glasses up higher on his nose. "What did we find?"

Already Landon was smiling. Kari took in the hill ahead of them and she shook her head. She definitely knew where this was going.

When all eyes were on her and everyone was listening, Ashley raised her voice. "Volcano, people!

We found an actual volcano!" She stomped her large shoes. "The ground is shaking, and look!" Ashley pointed up ahead. "See that smoke? The lava is about to erupt! We're right in the path!"

Mr. Garrett turned and looked in the direction where Ashley was pointing. He narrowed his eyes. "That?" He glanced at Ashley and back at the smoke ahead of them. "That isn't smoke, Ashley. It's fog.

Ashley stared at the fog for a few seconds. Then her arms fell to her sides. "Oh." She blinked. "But . . . the ground was shaking." She tapped the ground with the toe of Landon's shoe. A little softer this time. "Hey . . . it stopped shaking."

"The rumbling . . . that was a truck. There's a rock quarry not far from here." Mr. Garrett had a patient voice. "They go up and down the mountain all day moving rocks."

"Perhaps . . ." Ashley's eyes lit up, but only halfway this time. "That was a different volcano?"

"No, Ashley." Elliot stepped forward. "Indiana doesn't have volcanoes." He looked at the teacher. "Right, Mr. Garrett?"

The boys were all shaking their heads now. Same with Liza and Mandy and Natalie. Chris made a sour face. "You thought this was a volcano?"

Mr. Garrett gave the boy a stern look. "Chris."

He stepped back. "Sorry. It's just . . ."

"It's okay, Ashley." Landon gave Chris a friendly punch in the arm. "I could see where the fog and truck sounds, the hill . . . all of it could make this feel like a volcano."

"Thank you." Ashley held her head high. "I'm sure this place is very much like a real volcano."

"Okay, that's enough." Mr. Garrett turned and started up the hill again. "Let's keep moving."

They rounded a corner and right in front of them was a wide stream moving over and between the rocks. Also, a group of picnic tables sat not far from the water.

"For a minute"—Mr. Garrett turned to the kids—"I'd like you to just listen. Listen to the sound of being outdoors."

Kari closed her eyes. She heard the breeze in the tree branches above her and the sound of leaves brushing against each other. Also, the musical sound of water moving down the hillside. But that wasn't all. There was the chirp of birds overhead and the deep voice of a family of frogs not too far away.

Nature was alive with sounds . . . sounds she would have missed if it weren't for science camp!

She opened her eyes just as Mr. Garrett gave the next directions. "I'll set up a microscope on this table. Then each of you fill your beaker with water from the stream. You won't believe what you'll find!"

"Okay." Kari took hold of Ashley's arm. "Let's go."

Ashley stared at her. "Look at you! You actually sound happy about this."

"I am." Kari felt the thrill of all that was ahead. "I'm just glad we're not standing on a volcano!"

They both laughed and went to the water's edge with the others. They kneeled down and scooped their beakers into the stream. "It's cold." Kari was careful not to lean over too far. She filled her container and stood a few feet back. Ashley did the same.

Both girls held up the beakers and Kari frowned.

"Nothing. Not for you or for me. We found totally clear water." Kari shrugged at Ashley. "Let's try again. She started back toward the edge of the stream.

"Hold on, girls." Mr. Garrett was at the picnic table, his microscope set up. "That water isn't as clear as you think."

Kari and Ashley walked their beakers to Mr. Garrett. By now other kids were gathering around with their samples, too.

"We'll start with Kari." Mr. Garrett took her beaker. "All I need is a drop of your sample to prove the experiment. That life can be smaller than you might think."

Ashley's teacher used a small dropper to place a single dot of Kari's water onto a tiny clear glass square. Kari squinted at the drop. It wasn't much to look at. "Okay, Kari." Mr. Garrett motioned for her to come closer. He turned the microscope toward her. "Put your eye at the top here, then close the other eye. Twist the knob until the image is clear."

By now the entire group was gathered around,

each student holding a container from the stream. Mr. Garrett smiled at them. "A microscope lets you see things you can't see with the human eye. It's an amazing tool."

Kari held one eye up to the microscope and closed the other. She twisted the knob and then . . . "What in the world?" She stood straight again and stared at Mr. Garrett. "There's a whole world there! On that one drop of water."

Mr. Garrett nodded. "Take a closer look."

Once more Kari positioned herself over the microscope. Tiny beings were crawling and swimming, darting across the water and swimming across it. Almost like it was an entire lake instead of a single droplet.

"That's incredible." Kari looked at Mr. Garrett and then at her friends. "You have to see this!"

Next it was Ashley's turn. Mr. Garrett gave her a fresh glass square and took a drop from her sample. Ashley stared at it through the microscope. "Hey!" She glanced up and then back at her water drop. "There's a whole zoo in this thing!"

"Right!" Mr. Garrett smiled. "The created things

aren't just visible through our human eyes. That water looks clean enough to drink. But some of what you're looking at is bacteria, which means you'd have to boil the water before consuming it."

"Who knew?" Kari had never imagined anything like it. Her adventure reminders came back to her. Especially this one: Expect the unexpected. Because this unexpected treasure, the world that lived in a drop of water, was one she would remember forever. There would be more ahead, Kari was sure. And that made this adventure one she was more excited about than ever before.

When the kids in their group were finished with the microscope, Mr. Garrett instructed them to find a spot at one of the picnic tables. "Pull out your pencils and your experiment packet from your backpack." He told them to find the page that read, "What's in Stream Water?" Then they were each to write a paragraph about it and draw a picture showing what they saw in their droplets.

Not long after, Kari had written six sentences about what they had done this morning. Now she looked over at her sister's paper. Ashley had just three written sentences, but her drawings were spectacular.

Kari felt her shoulders slump forward. "Ashley, how do you draw so well?" Kari couldn't believe it. Ashley's drawings looked just like what they saw in the microscope. Like an exact copy.

"Well . . ." Ashley kept moving her pencil across her page. "A drawing is just how you see it in your head."

Kari liked the sound of that. It took away some of the pressure. She thought hard about a small wormy thing she had seen in her drop of water. She could draw that, definitely. The wormy thing grew clearer in her mind, and sure enough, a few minutes later the wormy thing was spread across her experiment paper. "I did it!"

Ashley looked over. "Yes, you did!"

By now, Mandy and Liza and Natalie had finished their written microscope observations and were working on their sketches.

"I couldn't believe how many things were crawling in that water." Liza shook her head. "Sort of gross."

"Not gross at all," Elliot called from the picnic

table near theirs. "Coolest thing I've ever seen!"

Mandy wrinkled her nose. "I'll stick to swimming pools from now on. At least I know there's no bacteria in there." She laughed.

Mr. Garrett was walking by their table and heard that. "Oh, there's bacteria in—"

"No!" Mandy covered her ears. "Don't tell me. I can't bear to know."

"That's why we have chlorine." Landon looked over at the girls. "Plus, a little bacteria never hurt anyone."

"Me and Elliot are the last of the group." Natalie walked over with Elliot. She plopped down on the log next to Ashley. "That was the craziest thing I've seen."

On the way back, Elliot was walking slower than usual. After a few minutes he stopped. "I don't feel so well . . ." He removed his glasses and dropped to a nearby rock.

"What's wrong?" Ashley stopped on one side of Elliot and Kari took the other side.

"Sometimes . . . I get low blood sugar." He hung his head. "When I've done a . . . lot of exercise."

"Wait!" Kari remembered the granola bar in her backpack. She took it out and handed it to Elliot. "Maybe this will help!"

"Thanks!" Elliot lifted his head. "I forgot mine." He took the bar, peeled back the wrapper and took a bite. "Yes. I'll feel better in no time."

After a minute they caught up with the rest of the group. Kari smiled to herself. This was another of her helpful adventure reminders. *Always be prepared*. She had done just that, and now things were fine with Elliot.

Adventures were definitely more fun with the reminders.

When they got back to camp they had lunch and then field races. The experiment was to carry various things across the field. The heavier the object, the slower the kids could run. "That's called gravitational pull," Ms. Nan told the fifth and sixth graders. "Every time you lift your leg you pull against gravity. The more weight you carry, the harder it is to get your foot off the ground."

Kari had never thought of that. A secret force working to keep you glued to the ground.

Finally, they had hamburgers around the campfire, and it was time for sleep already.

Even after the lights were out and the other girls were asleep, Kari was awake. She stared at the ceiling imagining invisible wormy things and a gravitational pull that worked against her with every step. It was a lot to think about.

The moonlight shone through the window near Kari's upper bunk. That didn't help. Also, it was freezing cold. She pulled her blanket up to her chin, but that didn't help.

"Are you awake?" Ashley whispered from the bed below Kari.

Kari sighed. "Yes. It's so cold." She sat up in her bed.

"Me too!" Ashley grunted. "It's like Mount Everest."

Just then Kari heard something outside. The sound sent shivers down her spine.

HowwwwwwHowwwwHowwww!

"Ashley! Do you hear that? It's wolves." Kari brought her knees up and hugged them close to her body.

"I hear it." Ashley was quiet.

Kari swallowed. "Definitely wolves."

"We're safe in here." Ashley didn't sound nervous.

After a while the howling stopped, but then . . . then there was a different sort of growling. And this one was coming from inside the cabin! "Ashley! What's that?"

This time Ashley scrambled to the top bunk and sat next to Kari. "It's a bear! It's . . . it's in the cabin! At the other end!"

What were they supposed to do? Kari hugged Ashley and the two tried not to move.

Very quietly Ashley whispered, "Maybe this is where we make friends with the wild bears?"

"No! We're in trouble!" Kari's heart was pounding now. "We need to wake up Ms. Nan!"

The problem was Ms. Nan's bunk was at the other end of the room with the parent chaperones.

And that was the exact place where the growling was coming from.

"Give me your flashlight!" Ashley held out her hand.

"Great idea." Kari had her flashlight beside her pillow. Just in case she had to get up in the middle of the night and use the bathroom. She handed it to Ashley.

The sound was getting louder.

Brave as could be, Ashley turned on the light. Then she aimed it at the far end of the room. After a few seconds, she clicked off. "It's not a bear." She giggled.

"What is it?" Kari could barely catch her breath. If it wasn't a bear, it must've been some other wild animal. Right here inside the cabin with the girls. "Is it a lion?"

"No." More giggling from Ashley. "It's one of the moms. She's snoring."

"Really?" Kari flopped back on her pillow and began to laugh, too. They both put their faces in Kari's pillow so their laughter wouldn't wake up the others. After a while, Kari yawned.

"I guess we can go to sleep now." She smiled at her younger sister.

Ashley nodded. "I'm tired. Plus . . . more adventuring tomorrow!"

Without any further laughter or conversation, and with the certainty that they weren't in danger, the girls finally fell asleep.

Kari could hardly wait for tomorrow. She had just one sad thought before she fell asleep.

Science camp was going way too fast!

16

Two Smooth Stones

ASHLEY

At breakfast, the snoring mom sat with Ashley and Kari and the other girls. She was the mom of Sofia in Ashley's class. And she was really nice.

Which made Ashley smile to herself. Because they had made friends with a wild bear, after all. She kept this happy detail to herself. Sofia's mother might not want to be thought of as a bear.

"Attention, students!" Mr. Garrett stood at the front of the cafeteria and spoke through a megaphone. "We have a full day planned. We will begin by studying birdcalls."

"Yes!" Elliot was at the next table with the boys. He stood up and rubbed his hands together. "I love birdcalls." He looked around to whoever was listening. "I have twenty-two birdcalls memorized. In case anyone needs help today."

Mr. Garrett seemed to wait for Elliot to sit down again. "Now . . . in a moment, Ms. Nan will play recordings of birdcalls. Then we will head out into the woods in our groups and try to find birds who make the same sound. You can also identify them by their markings and physical attributes. Photos and descriptions of birds are in your packets." Mr. Garrett held up the packet turned to the correct page. "Good luck and have fun!"

Within minutes, Ashley and her group were back outside. Mr. Garrett was with them again, and as soon as they were alone in the woods, Elliot held up his hand. "Listen!" His voice was a loud whisper. Do you hear it?"

Ashley listened with all her strength. But all she could hear was the wind in the trees. And the squeak of a little chipmunk, maybe.

"There it is again!" Elliot's eyes grew wide. "That's a brown-headed nuthatch." He turned to their teacher. "Right, Mr. Garrett?"

Mr. Garrett looked at the packet in his hands and then back at Elliot. "I'm going to have to take your word on that." He chuckled. "Okay, everyone. Put a check mark next to the brown-headed nuthatch.

Ashley couldn't believe it. She'd lived all her life right into the fifth grade and she'd never heard of a brown-headed nuthatch. "How did you know, Elliot?"

"Yeah, how did you know?" Landon walked up. He scratched his head.

"Because." Elliot smiled at the friends gathered around. "They sound a little like a chipmunk in distress."

"I knew it!" Ashley flapped her arms and marched in a small circle. "*Squa-squa-squa!* I actually thought it was a chipmunk." She looked at Elliot again. "In distress, of course." Ashley kept flapping and making the birdcall.

"Wow." Elliot grinned at her. "That's pretty close, Ashley."

"Yes." Chris laughed. "I'd say you are a very convincing brown-headed nuthatch, Ashley."

"Hmm." Ashley studied that laughing Chris. "Do you mean it?"

"I really do." Chris looked at Landon and Elliot. "Can we all agree? Ashley is definitely a perfect brown-headed nuthatch."

"All right." Mr. Garrett motioned for them to keep moving. "Let's see if we can hear any other birds."

An hour later they had identified eleven of the birds on the list, mostly because of Elliot. Before they made it back to camp a screaming sound pierced the forest. Ashley grabbed hold of Kari and Natalie. Liza and Mandy quickly joined their little group.

"Mr. Garrett!" Ashley whispered. "Help! Someone is being attacked. Probably by a lion!"

"No!" Elliot motioned for them to be quiet again. "Listen!" His face lit up. "That's a red-tailed hawk! I've never seen one in person! Where is it?"

Everyone in the group turned their attention to the trees, looking for any sign of the bird.

"What does he look like?" Liza shouted, a little too loud for the quiet bird-watching woods.

"I see it. Over there!" Kari pointed up to the trees.

Ashley whipped her head around and her jaw dropped. She had never seen anything so regal and majestic. The hawk looked kind of like pictures she had seen of bald eagles. It opened its wings and flapped them a few times from the branch it was sitting on

"Wow. Look at that." Elliot dropped to the ground, his mouth open. "A real, live red-tailed hawk!"

The friends followed Elliot's example. Even Mr. Garrett sat on the ground and watched the hawk. After a minute of flapping and crying out, the hawk flapped its massive wings three times and flew away.

Off through the Indiana woods.

"Clarence!" Ashley stood and called after the bird. "Come back!"

"Clarence?" Natalie stood and crossed her arms. "You named the hawk Clarence?"

"Yes!" Ashley didn't want to lose the bird. She thought she could keep up. She bolted away from the others, her eyes glued on the hawk. One large shoe foot after the other, pushing against gravity, Ashley ran.

Somewhere in the back of her head she could hear Mr. Garrett and the others calling her, but she couldn't stop running. Even in Landon's floppy sneakers. Ashley just had to keep up with Clarence.

"I'm coming, Clarence!" she called out. The bird had her full attention. Which meant the ground she was running on clearly did not. Ashley didn't care. She kept running, tripping over rocks and sticks and leaves. Kept pushing herself until—

"Waaaaaa!" Ashley's foot hit nothing but air. She began to roll and tumble down a cliffy hill and then—*Splat!* She landed flat in a small stream. Her next few breaths didn't feel quite right, and something else.

Ashley had lost Clarence.

She smacked her hands against the water, but she needed all her effort for breathing. Finally, she sat up and stared at her wet arms and legs. She could breathe again, which was nice. But so much invisible bacteria! Ashley forced herself not to think about it. "H-h-help!"

"Ashley!" Kari shouted.

"Where are you?" It was Mr. Garrett's voice this time. "Ashley Baxter?"

"H-h-here! Off the c-c-cliff!" She finally yelled loud enough for them to hear her.

First came Kari's face, then her teacher's. Then Landon and Chris and Elliot, Natalie and Liza and Mandy. The whole group was standing at the top of the drop-off staring at her.

Landon started to scramble down the cliff, but Mr. Garrett stopped him. "We don't need two students stuck in the ravine." He took his backpack from his shoulders and rummaged around inside. "Here!" It was a long section of thick white rope. "We'll need to work as a team." Then he looked at Ashley. "How do you feel?"

"Sad." Ashley wanted to be honest. "I almost caught that hawk, Mr. Garrett. I was so close."

Her teacher shook his head. "No, I mean how do your arms and legs feel? What about your head?"

"Oh." Ashley felt her hands and feet, her knees, and ribs. "I'm fine I think." She noticed a cut on her elbow. "Except this." She held it up so Mr.

Garrett could see it. "And also the invisible bacteria. That's the worst of it."

"You don't have a headache?" He seemed more worried than usual.

"No." She shook her head a few times just to be sure. "Nope. Just a bloody elbow and a whole lot of bacteria."

"Okay." Mr. Garrett turned to the boys. "We're going to make a human chain and get her up that way."

"A what?" Ashley stood, but her floppy shoes brought her smack back down into the stream.

"I'll go first." Landon raised his hand.

Then like trained survival experts, Mr. Garrett and the boys tied one end of the rope to Landon's waist. All of them took hold of the rope and slowly they lowered Landon down to where Ashley lay in the stream.

Before he reached her, Ashley blinked hard a few times. In case maybe this was a bad dream, and she could wake up. Because this was the most embarrassing thing she'd done since starting fifth grade. Nothing else was close.

"Here." Landon held out his hand. "Stand up but take your time." He grinned at her. "I'm going to need those shoes back at the end of the trip."

"Fine." Ashley had no choice. She took Landon's hand and stood. Her knees were shaky, and her clothes were wet. But with Mr. Garrett and the boys all pulling on the rope, Landon helped her up the rocky cliff in no time.

Once she reached the top, Kari handed her a napkin from her backpack. "To wipe the bacteria from your face." She managed a slight smile. "I'm so sorry, Ashley."

"It's my fault." Ashley felt sore and she would need a bandage for her elbow. "Gravity won this time around."

"Yes." Mr. Garrett chuckled. "I guess it did. You're sure you're okay?"

Ashley was finished talking about the fall. For the rest of her life, she would pretend it never happened. Even though her sweatshirt and jeans were dripping with stream water. She cleared her voice. "Honestly, Mr. Garrett, I would just like to get back to camp to see if our group had the most birdcalls. Clarence put us over the edge, I believe."

They all nodded, and Mr. Garrett put away the rope.

Landon pulled something from his backpack and handed it to Ashley. "It's a Band-Aid." He took off the paper backing and put it on her elbow. "So you don't get blood on my shoes."

Ashley almost laughed. Almost. When the bandage was in place, she looked at Landon. "Thank you. For saving my life . . . and for the Band-Aid."

A grin tugged at that boy's lips. "You're welcome. Was Clarence worth it?"

"Yes." Ashley gave a single nod. "He most definitely was."

On the way back to camp, Kari came up alongside her. "Never do that again." She shook her head at Ashley. "You have to watch where you're going."

"You know what it was?" Ashley pointed at her shoes. "Clown shoes. That's what."

They made it back for lunch and indeed, Mr. Garrett's team had heard the most birdcalls. Ashley wasn't surprised. "Way to go, Elliott!" She gave her friend a high five.

For their last activity of the day, Mr. Garrett explained he was going to choose pairs of names from a bag to make partners for this activity. "Together you will find something unique from the forest. A discovery. Then tonight you and your teammate will share that discovery around the campfire."

The first two names were Natalie and Elliot. Then Chris and Mandy. After that came Kari and Liza. Ashley felt herself sinking into the ground. Only this time it wasn't gravity making her want to hide.

"Ashley Baxter." Mr. Garrett held up her name. "You will be with . . . Landon Blake. Landon? Where are you?"

"Over here." Landon's voice rang out from the table across from Ashley's. He caught Ashley's eyes and waved. Just a slight lift of the hand.

Ashley shrugged. At least Landon was her friend. Plus, he had saved her life earlier, in the Clarence disaster.

"Hey." Ashley gave him a thumbs-up. "You ready to find the best object in the woods?"

"Yeah." Landon put his hands in his pockets. "We'll be a good team. Let's go." He gestured to the door and the two of them led the others out of the cafeteria.

Each team of two had to stay in an area blocked off for this next adventure, so no one would get lost. Ashley and Landon walked for a while in silence. Admiring the nature. Listening for Clarence.

Ashley spoke first. "So . . . how have you been, Landon? I feel like we haven't caught up in a bit. Not really since the play."

"Yeah. I guess not. I'm good." Landon kept his eyes forward. "You've been doing, okay? Other than . . . you know." He smiled at her.

"Right." She rubbed her elbow. "That." She laughed, first time since her fall. "Yes, I'm good. I've been looking forward to this for so long."

"This?" Landon sounded surprised.

"Not this. Not the walk with you." Ashley looked at her big shoes. "No, I mean science camp."

"Yeah, me, too." He took a deep breath and smiled. "I like being outside." Landon always seemed sure of himself.

"You did great in the play, by the way." She kept her eyes on the ground. So far she hadn't seen any great discovery. "You know what?"

"What?" Landon was still smiling.

Ashley stopped walking and looked at him. "I didn't think you'd be a very great Captain Hook, Landon. But you were. You were believable."

"Thanks." He laughed. "I think." He walked a bit more. "And I liked how you played Wendy. Taking control of the ship and staying in Neverland!"

"Are you making fun of me, Landon Blake?" Ashley put her hands on her hips.

Landon shook his head. "No. It was very entertaining. I mean it."

They made their way down a trail and Ashley pointed to a spot just ahead. "Another creek. Maybe there's something in there."

"Hey, there!" Natalie called out from behind them. She and Elliot hurried to catch up to them. "Look what we found!"

Elliot had never looked happier. He held up a grayish white stick. "Can you believe it? This is an old animal bone!"

"Uh. Guys . . . I hate to ruin this party but . . ." Landon sounded a little nervous. He hopped away. Moving his legs around.

Ashley patted his arm. "Relax, Landon. We'll find our objects, don't worry." She studied him. "Also, what dance is that?"

"It's . . . not a dance!" He pointed to the hill they'd been standing on. "That's an anthill!"

Ashley looked down and saw a hundred little ants racing up her legs and into her clown shoes. "Yikes!" She screamed and jumped off the hill. Natalie and Elliot did the same thing.

The four of them danced and hopped and swiped at the ants. Ashley sat on an old log and dumped each ant from Landon's sneakers until finally the four of them were bug free.

Elliot bent over his knees, out of breath. "Good news. These are not poisonous red ants. These are brown." He slipped his shoes back on. "Thankfully."

"But they're still . . . ants," Natalie whimpered. "I think I've had enough."

"We should get back anyway." Elliot helped

Natalie to her feet. "We've already found our object."

"Landon and I will meet up with you later." Ashley waved at Natalie and Elliot. This was another science camp adventure she could have skipped. Who wants to get covered up by ants?

"It was kind of funny." Landon shrugged, "Anyway . . . we should check the stream. Either that or we'll have to talk about your wet clothes. And how you fell over the cliff chasing Clarence."

Ashley's face felt hot. "We definitely need to find something else."

They walked to the stream's edge and ran their hands in the water, picking up things from the bottom. Landon pulled up some moss. Ashley found a plastic bottle, which she put in her backpack. "Because trash shouldn't be in mountain streams."

"True. Look!" Landon held up a stone. "It's so smooth."

Ashley dug her hand in the creek and pulled out one just like it. "Wow. It *is* smooth."

"My dad told me that stones get smooth in rivers and creeks because of the sand and dirt and water pressure. The faster it runs over them, the more smooth they become. He said it's like when we go through a hard time or a tough season."

"Pressure makes beautiful things." Ashley continued the thought.

"Yep. I think this is the perfect object." Landon tossed the stone in the air and tucked it in his pocket. "Two smooth stones. That's perfect." He looked toward camp. "Let's go. We don't want to be late."

As they walked back to the cafeteria, Ashley thought about what Landon had said. How pressure can bring beauty. Like Meena and her family, who had gone through so much pain and hard times. But their life was smoother now and it was beautiful—maybe even because of the hard times.

Then she thought about Joseph from the Bible. He was under a lot of pressure. He even got put in prison for doing nothing wrong. But in the end, his life was beautiful and smooth. It just took time.

Landon was right. These stones were the perfect objects to present tonight. Because they were an illustration for what Ashley had been learning in life. Hard times and pressure not only made for beautiful stones.

They made for beautiful people, too.

At least with the two smooth stones, she wouldn't have to talk about chasing Clarence and falling down the cliff. Because that would only remind Chris of the obvious.

Deep down, Ashley really was a brown-headed nuthatch.

She smiled. She would draw herself as that bird when she got home from science camp.

Because if she were completely honest with herself, the name actually fit.

17

Mac and Feathers

KARI

Kari grabbed her jacket from her bunk, slipped it on, and headed out for the campfire that night. Ashley and Liza were with her, so they grabbed theirs, too.

"See?" Ashley spun around. "This rainbow jacket is my raincoat of many colors!"

"Yes." Liza smiled. "It is definitely that." She looked up at the sky and the other girls did the same. "No rain tonight, though."

"Nope." Kari was glad because rain on the bonfire wouldn't be great.

As they hurried toward the open field where the bonfire was taking place, a boy named Mac from the class across the hall from Kari caught up with them. "It's cold tonight." He zipped his sweatshirt. "Science camp has been great, right?"

"The best!" Kari meant it. Even after Ashley's fall, the day had still been so fun.

"And look." Liza held up a speckled feather. "Kari and I found this in the forest. It's our special discovery."

Mac nodded. "I like it."

"So, Mac." Ashley stepped up. "How's that magic act going?"

Kari shot her a look. It said that Ashley better be nice to Mac. The fact that his talent show act had been a flop didn't mean she needed to bring it up.

Mac laughed. "Oh, that. Yeah, not great."

"I remember your tryout." Kari turned to Mac. "It wasn't bad, really. Just a bit of a . . ." Kari stopped herself. What positive thing could she really say about Mac's magic act?

"It was a train wreck." Mac shook his head. He was still laughing. "I never practiced."

"I wondered." Kari and Liza swapped a smile. But only because Mac could laugh at himself. Kari looked at the boy again. "Did you ever get your sleeve fixed? From when it ripped off?"

"You can laugh, it's okay." Mac seemed to understand he was probably never going to be a famous magician. "You're Kari, right? You were in the dancing group."

"We were." She pointed to Liza. "The two of us and our friend Mandy."

"'Under the Sea' it was called." Ashley danced her way ahead of the group. A fish-type dance where she weaved one way then the other with her hand up near her head. Like a fin. Only she danced backward into a tall bushy weed and got white dust all over her sweatshirt.

Ashley spun around and faced the group. "See, Mac? Kari gets her dancing skills from me."

Mac gave Ashley a thumbs-up. Then he smiled at Kari. "You girls did great."

"What about me?" Ashley stopped her fish dance. "I was Wendy, you know."

"Wendy?" Maybe Mac had been out of the room for that part. Because no one could've forgotten Ashley Baxter's Wendy.

"Yes!" Ashley took hold of the captain's wheel

246

of an invisible ship. Then she raised her imaginary sword. "Back to Neverland!" She stared at Mac. "Don't you remember?"

"Oh, yeah! You were in the Peter Pan play."

"Exactly." Ashley brushed at some of the white weed dust on her sweatshirt. "That Wendy."

They reached the bonfire area and Mac spotted his group. "See you later!" He waved at Kari and Ashley and Liza and ran to his spot on the opposite side of the fire pit.

Kari and the girls found seats with their group.

Tonight they would each roast hot dogs over one of the small grills nearby. The teachers and parent volunteers were already set up near each cook station. Kari followed Ashley to the long folding tables that had the food supplies. Hot dogs, buns, potato chips, ketchup, mustard, and a dozen other hot dog toppings.

"This is a feast!" Elliot grabbed a hot dog and placed it on a stick.

Ms. Nan gave instructions through the megaphone. "Get a hot dog, then head to a cook station. One of the adults will help you cook your hot dog. And please . . . be careful."

Kari took her hot dog to Ms. Nan's grill. Her teacher helped her position the metal stick just right, so the hot dog stayed over the small flame. Natalie and Ashley joined her, and soon they were all three cooking hot dogs.

Like wilderness people.

"Speaking of science." Ms. Nan pointed to the grill. "Fire is the result of a chemical reaction." She helped Natalie move her hot dog closer to the flames. "To get fire you need fuel, oxygen, and heat."

"You mean, like, the wood in the grill?" Kari thought she understood. "That's the fuel?"

"Right." Ms. Nan smiled. She clearly loved this science stuff. "And the air around us, that's the oxygen. Then all you need is a spark."

"That's me." Ashley twirled her cold hot dog near the top of the fire. "I'm a human spark, Ms. Nan."

"I can see that." Kari's teacher grinned. "But fire needs a different kind of spark." She adjusted Ashley's stick, so the hot dog was actually in the flame. "The spark is the heat. Usually a very small flame. But the spark might also come from clicking two sharp stones together. When the spark connects with the fuel and oxygen, the atoms rearrange themselves irreversibly." She held her hands up. "And just like that . . . fire!"

Kari noticed that her hot dog was sizzling. She pulled it close and examined it. Perfectly crisp. She walked by herself to the table and watched people building their hot dogs. Elliot loaded his up with chili and onions and relish, and Chris crushed chips on his. But Kari went with something simpler.

She grabbed the ketchup bottle just as Mac walked up with his dinner plate.

He pointed to Kari's hot dog. "Can't go wrong with ketchup and mustard."

Kari held her hot dog up. "I always love the classic."

"I'm more complex. Like my magic tricks." Mac grabbed a spoon of the chili and tried to fling it on his hot dog. Only instead, it flung backward. All over his face and shirt.

Kari gasped. "Oh no!" She grabbed a nearby napkin. "Here."

"And he does it again." Mac laughed, teasing himself. He rubbed the napkin over the chili spots, but that only spread the stain. Mac shrugged. "I guess I'm a mess."

"Kind of like your hot dog." Kari noticed that he had already stuffed it with so many things.

"Looks like I need a new shirt!" He laughed again, grabbed his plate and headed off.

"Kari. Come on, let's find a seat. They're about to get started!" Liza nudged Kari's elbow.

"Science camp has been so fun!" Mandy walked up. "And now my favorite dinner!"

"It's way better than I thought it would be." Kari walked with the girls to one of the outdoor tables. Ashley and the boys from their group were already there.

After dinner all the fifth and sixth graders sat around the bonfire. Mr. Garrett had the megaphone this time. "Welcome to the final night of science camp!" the teacher's voice rang out. "You've all made exciting discoveries today, and this is your chance to share those discoveries with your classmates."

Mr. Garrett explained how they would do more in-depth presentations of their objects once they were back at school. "So hang on to your item." Ashley's teacher looked at the various groups of kids around the bonfire. Then he held up a microphone. "Who would like to go first?"

Chris and Mandy stood and walked up to Mr. Garrett. Mandy took the microphone. "We found a magical stick with moss growing on it. It looks like a mini-forest all on one stick."

Next up were Kari and Liza. They shared their feather, and Kari pointed out that the thing was almost longer than her arm. "We think it was from a red-tailed hawk." Kari grinned at Ashley in the audience. "A hawk named Clarence."

Other kids took their turns sharing discoveries of a robin's nest, a basket of colorful leaves, an enormous walnut, and a small snake in a bucket.

Ms. Nan ran up to those students and took the bucket from them. The three of them hurried off. Probably because they weren't supposed to pick up live animals.

When the students were done talking about their discoveries, Ms. Nan found Kari and Liza. "I love your feather, girls."

Kari had it now. She held it over to Ms. Nan. "It's so long, right?"

"It is." Her teacher studied the feather. "That's a flight feather. I agree . . . probably from a hawk." Ms. Nan put her hand on Kari's shoulder. "Very impressive."

"Thanks." Kari felt her heart burst with pride. "It's the most beautiful thing we could find."

As Ms. Nan walked away, Kari was proud of herself. She had done it! She had expected the unexpected—seeing little swimmy things in the stream water. And she had embraced the surprises—when Ashley forgot her shoes. And she had tried new things—like listening to birdcalls. She was even prepared when Elliot needed a snack.

She had come to science camp and tackled the challenges. Best of all, she'd had fun doing it.

Kari smiled. No wonder her siblings liked adventures.

Mr. Garrett closed out the night. "Thanks for

sharing tonight, boys and girls." He waited a moment for the crowd to get quiet again. "Nature is special. And we are just visitors here. We have to always remember to respect the earth and protect it."

"I like this," Mandy whispered to Kari. "He's right about the earth."

Kari nodded, but she kept her eyes on the teacher. Mr. Garrett turned his eyes to the sky and then to the distant trees, and finally back at the students. "God's beauty is everywhere. Which is why the goal of these few days was to get you to spend time outdoors. To see that creation and science are all around us."

Mr. Garrett picked up his guitar and led the group in a song about taking care of creation and spending time in nature.

During the song, Kari stared at the trees and the crackling fire. She felt the wind and she thought of Clarence the hawk and the atoms and the smallest unseen things in life. These few days weren't just about science. They were about God and everything He had created.

"Before you go back to your cabins, sit on the

grass for a while. Notice the sky. The stars and the moon." Mr. Garrett looked up again. "And remember no matter where you are, you can always step outside and be a part of nature."

When Mr. Garrett turned off the megaphone, the students moved to the grass, where they sat in circles. As if each of them was suddenly more aware of the stars than ever before. Like there was something very special about this night and this place.

Kari leaned back on her hands, staring at the sky. This was almost like when she and her family had watched the meteor shower not too long ago. "It's beautiful out here." Kari's voice was quiet.

"It's like we're in God's house." Ashley leaned against her sister.

Just then a shooting star arced across the speckled night sky. *God,* Kari thought, *You let me see a shooting star. Thank You!*

A shooting star might have been a small thing. But it mattered to her. Which meant it mattered to God, too.

Later, when Kari and the other girls walked back to their cabin, Kari felt different than before science camp. She was wonderstruck, but not just at the creation. At the Creator.

Easily the best Scientist there was.

18

Science Camp Sunrise

ASHLEY

All adventures had to end.

And that's exactly why Ashley hated to see this morning come. After so much waiting and excitement, science camp was over. It was more adventuring than she could have expected or hoped for. And, while she would never say so to her neighbor friend Marsha, science camp was definitely better than a cruise.

Still, Ashley had one more thing she wanted to do before they left.

She climbed out of her bunk bed before the rest of her cabin was awake, just as the sun was coming up. Then she slipped into Landon's oversized sneakers, grabbed her sketchbook and tiptoed outside.

Other than the drawings they had to do in their packets, Ashley hadn't done much sketching over the last few days. She needed to capture something while she was still out here.

Ashley caught a whiff of her clothes. They smelled like campfire, but she didn't mind. The scent brought back memories from last night.

Every moment of the last few days was a top shelf experience.

Ashley liked this saying because it was reserved for only the best of times. Like how Mom's china, the best dishes, was reserved for the top shelf. So, when something was extra good or special, lately Ashley called it a top-shelf experience.

She found a chair just outside the cabin door and she faced a line of trees not far away. The smallest sliver of sun was lifting into the sky. Ashley pulled out her pencils and turned to the next blank page.

The final thing Ashley wanted to see before she left science camp was this: a sunrise.

She focused on the tree line first and she began to draw. Each tree was a different height and shape, so she was careful to get each one in her drawing just right.

Next she sketched the grass. And finally, Ashley added the lines of the sunrise—pinks and yellows and pale blues. Every minute the sunrise grew brighter and more colorful, so she had to work fast.

Ashley looked down at her work and her heart felt warm. This was her most beautiful picture, yet. She was sure.

Finally, she added her own special touch to the sketch. In the corner of the page, Ashley drew a volcano. The one she never got to see on this trip. Also, a small, but friendly, wild bear. Because even though she hadn't seen those things, they were in her mind, where they would stay. Whenever she thought about fifth-grade science camp.

"Good morning!" Elliot called out from behind her.

"Hi." Ashley turned to see Elliot standing there, his backpack on and duffel bag in hand. "You're already packed?"

"Yep. We have a late breakfast and then the bus.

Doesn't make sense to wait." Elliot sat in the chair next to Ashley. "What are you doing?"

"Drawing the sunrise. Before it's gone." Ashley handed him her sketchbook.

Elliot's jaw dropped. "I don't know how you do it, Ashley. But you are by far the best artist ever."

"Thanks, Elliot." Ashley took the sketchbook back.

"And I should know." Elliot reached into his bag and pulled out the comic book Ashley had made for him. "I've got my own personal Ashley Baxter artwork right here. It's really good. Like . . . out of all the comics I've read, it's the best."

"Thanks, Elliot." Ashley smiled at him. This crazy fun classmate of hers had really become one of her best friends. Everyone needed an Elliot in their life. And Ashley was thankful she had him.

"I guess I should pack, too." Ashley stood and gathered her colored pencils. "See you at break-fast."

"Oh, I'll be there. Plus, I've been warming up my voice for the bus ride home." Elliot clapped his hands a few times. "The kids love it!"

"Yes, they do." Ashley grinned at him. "Can't wait."

Before going back inside the cabin, Ashley found a handful of acorns and orange and red leaves, funny-shaped rocks, pointy feathers. Items to share with Brooke and Erin and Luke back at home. When she returned to her bunk, she stuffed them into her bag.

On her bed was one of the smooth rocks she had found with Landon. She tucked that into her pocket, where she knew it would be safe. Memories for another day. Also, they still had to talk about that discovery in class next week.

Next, she removed Landon's sneakers and slipped her ballet shoes back on. On her elbow was the Band-Aid and she noticed a bruise on her lower leg, probably from falling off the cliff. She smiled. What a sight that must have been for the others in her group. She'd have to ask Kari about that later.

Anyway, she didn't mind a few scrapes and bruises from science camp.

They were proof of a good time. Because she had been a true adventurer despite the struggles.

With her bags packed and Landon's old shoes tucked under her arm, Ashley headed toward the exit door of the mostly empty cabin.

"Goodbye, cabin. I hope you have kids as good as us next time around." She walked out the door and made her way to the cafeteria.

Most of the fifth and sixth graders were cleaning

up and heading to the buses. So, Ashley helped herself to a bowl of cereal from the incredible table-long display of boxes and hurried to her table.

"Two minutes!" Mr. Garrett stepped into the cafeteria and looked straight at Ashley. "Don't be late to the bus!"

Ashley raised her spoon. She had too many Cheerios in her mouth to talk. *Faster,* she told herself. *Eat faster.* She couldn't miss the bus, no matter what. How would she survive in the wilderness with only her smooth rock and Landon's big shoes? She chewed faster still.

"Hey!" Landon took the seat across from her. He watched her eat for a moment. "What's your hurry?"

Ashley sat up straighter and tried to move the cereal around in her mouth, but it made her cheeks very full. Too full to talk right. "Hewwo. . ." Her voice was muffled, and a bit of milk trickled down her chin and onto her sweatshirt. She wiped at it before Landon could notice. She kept chomping until she could speak clearly. "I don't want to miss the bus. Here." She grabbed his shoes and handed them over. "Thanks again . . . for these."

"Anytime. I bet you don't forget your shoes again." He got up and took a few steps toward the door. "See you on the bus."

"See ya." Ashley watched Landon go. He was a good friend. Science camp had proved that again. She finished her cereal and ran for the bus. Mr. Garrett was standing at the door with his clipboard.

"Well, Ashley." He smiled. "How was it?"

"The best." She grinned. "Even without the volcano." A wave of sadness hit her. "I will miss Clarence, though. And the brown-headed nuthatch."

"Yes." Mr. Garrett nodded at her. "I think we all will."

Ashley climbed on the bus and noticed something. The teachers and parent volunteers looked happy, but tired. Like Mr. Garrett. They'd worked hard to make science camp happen and Ashley decided it was time to give them some appreciation.

She stopped just past the teachers and parents

and raised her hands. "Attention, fifth and sixth graders." The kids on the bus stopped talking and looked at her. She had that effect on people. Ashley cleared her throat. "I believe it is time to thank the adults on the bus." With that, she turned around and began clapping. Soon, every student on the bus did the same thing. They cheered so loud Ashley figured somewhere in the sky, Clarence could've heard them.

Mr. Garrett waited for the applause to die down and for Ashley to take her seat. "Thank you, students. We appreciate you." Mr. Garrett gave the students two thumbs-up. "Now, everyone settle in. We'll be back at school in a little over four hours."

The bus ride home was a lively one. An hour in, Ashley stood and reenacted her fall down the cliff—for the kids who hadn't heard about it. Most of them looked alarmed, but a few clapped for her.

And, of course, the trip ended with Elliot singing another round of "Ninety-Nine Bottles of Milk in the Fridge." This time the whole bus sang along.

After another hour Liza stood and shouted, "We're home! There's the school." That announcement brought another roaring round of applause. They had made it home from the wilderness, back from bears and wolves, and hills like volcanoes. Back from anthills and tricky cliffs and snoring parent volunteers.

Back from the best weekend of fifth grade.

Ashley and Kari got off the bus, waved goodbye to their friends and ran for their mom. She stood by the car, arms wide open.

"Mom!" Ashley's heart felt warm and full. She'd missed her mom and dad and her siblings. It was good to be home.

Mom hugged them both tight. "Welcome back!"

"We had the best time, Mom," Kari squealed.

Mom raised her eyebrows. "You did? That's great to hear."

"I was prepared." Kari tapped Mom's shoulder. "Like you taught me to be."

"And what about you, Ash?" Mom ran her fingers through Ashley's hair. "Had a good time?"

"A great time. I have a lot of stories to tell you." Ashley tossed her bags in the car.

"How about we start with your shoes . . . why are you wearing *those*?" Mom pointed at Ashley's ballet slippers.

"Mom." Ashley laughed. "It's a long story."

"Can't wait to hear." Mom helped the girls with their things.

"Let me tell you about my time first." Kari sat in the front next to their mother. "We found a huge feather yesterday. And Ms. Nan said it was a flight feather . . ." Kari kept talking.

But Ashley turned her attention out the window. She buckled her seatbelt and watched Mr. Garrett saying goodbye to Landon and Elliot. Their teacher looked at Ashley and smiled as they drove off. She waved back.

Just then, Ashley saw another red-tailed hawk. She was certain, without a doubt, that it was Clarence. He had followed them home. He must have seen her fall and felt bad about it and now he was watching out for her. Making sure she was okay. Ashley would draw that bird later!

She sighed and settled into her seat.

With science camp behind her, Ashley was ready for her next adventure. Whatever it might be. Because every day as Ashley Baxter was an unforgettable adventure. And character awards were coming right up.

Ashley couldn't wait for that.

267

19

Finishing the List

KARI

W e're home!" Kari plopped her bags on the floor in the entryway. The smell of Dad's chicken soup filled the house. Mom hung up her coat and Ashley set her things down by the stairs. Kari did a sigh of relief.

She was back!

"Yay! You're here!" Erin came running up. She hugged Kari and then Ashley.

"Were you waiting for us?" Kari smiled at their youngest sister.

"Yes." Erin jumped a few times. "I missed you!"

"Welcome back!" Brooke shouted from the top of the stairs. She ran down and wrapped Kari in a big hug. "You survived!" She looked at Ashley. "Oh no . . . that Band-Aid."

"Not to worry." Ashley stood a little taller. "I survived, too." She unzipped her backpack. "Also . . . I have souvenirs for everyone."

"You made it!" Luke rounded the corner and slid on the hardwood in his socks, bumping into the sisters.

"Yes!" Kari patted Luke's hair. "Luke. You are going to love science camp when you get to go."

Ashley passed out her souvenirs. "An acorn for Luke. A rock for Erin. And a leaf. For Brooke." Ashley rocked back and forth on her toes humming.

Everyone seemed impressed. Kari held up her hands. "I didn't bring you anything. But I have lots of stories!"

Dad rounded the corner drying his hands on a towel. "My girls are back!"

Kari and Ashley ran to Dad and embraced him. "We got to use microscopes!" Kari stepped to the side. "Like real scientists!"

"I can't wait to hear about it." Dad directed

them to the dinner table. "This will be one special dinner."

They all headed for the dinner table and took a seat. Bo took his place near Luke's feet, hopeful that a scrap would fall on the ground.

"Hi, boy." Kari petted their dog's head. "I missed you."

Luke pointed to the corner of the room, where a dog bed was. "Bo. Back!"

The dog walked backward until he stood on the bed.

"Now sit." Luke moved his hand down toward the ground.

Bo sat. His ears stayed perked up as he tilted his head from side to side.

"Wow." Kari raised her eyebrows. "Impressive." The boys had obviously been busy during the last few days, too!

"Dad and I are training him." Luke stuck his chin in the air.

"So . . ." Mom dished salad onto her plate and passed the bowl. "Tell us how it was. Start from the beginning."

Kari told them about the bus ride and the cafeteria and the cabin and the wolf howling. She didn't miss a single detail.

"What about you, Ashley?" Her dad sat on the other side of the table. "How was science camp for you? And tell us about that bandage."

"Yes," Ashley nodded. She looked like she was trying to decide what to share. At least here, in front of everyone. She looked around the table. "I forgot my shoes. The adventure started there for me."

"What?" Brooke set her spoon down. "You can't forget your shoes to science camp."

"I did, though." Ashley nodded firmly. She lifted one slipper foot up and set it on the edge of the kitchen table. "I wore just these Wendy ballet slippers. That's it."

"Why?" Erin sat back in her chair and giggled. "You didn't bring your boots?"

Kari had asked the same question when they first got to camp. She smiled and shook her head at her goofy sister.

"Hmm." Mom didn't seem as amused. "I

remember asking you to pack your boots. And even an extra pair of sneakers."

Ashley took her foot off the table. She tapped her knee a few times. "I meant to obey, Mother. Really, I did. I never meant to be audacious."

Dad tried not to smile. He really did. But a small laugh escaped from him.

"You can't help it, Ashley." Kari laughed, too. "You are audacious. You take bold risks."

"True." Mom sat back in her chair. She didn't look too upset. "We just want you to obey first. Then be audacious."

Kari looked at her sister. Ashley seemed to think about whether that was possible.

Finally she nodded once. With emphasis. "Yes, Mom. I think I can do that." Ashley looked serious. "I'm really sorry. Plus, the true story is that Landon had an extra pair of long clown shoes for me. So, as it turned out, I was in good hands."

"Good feet," Luke said. "You were in good *feet* because of Landon's shoes."

They all laughed and then Dad looked at Kari. "What was your favorite part?"

Kari thought about that. How could she pick just one thing? Then she remembered. "One night we saw a shooting star. It was like a smile from God."

"Mmmm. God is good at that." Mom smiled. "Using small things to make us feel loved."

"Ashley?" Dad turned his attention to her. He had happy eyes. "What about you? Besides the slippers you wore to science camp."

"I think . . ." Ashley sucked in a long breath. "I'd have to say chasing after Clarence. The red-tailed hawk." She raised her eyebrows. "He followed us all the way back to school!"

Then Ashley told their family all about running after the hawk and naming him and falling down over the cliff. She touched her elbow. "That's why I have this Band-Aid. Also other bruises."

Kari glanced at the others. "What did you all do?"

"We had pizza!" Erin giggled. "Not cinna-noodles."

"And we played Go Fish!" Brooke patted Erin's hand. "You won, remember?"

273

"I did." Erin laughed. "I think I'm good at that card game."

"Then we had an adventure walk around the backyard and me and Brooke and Erin played H-O-R-S-E around the basketball hoop." Luke puffed out his chest. "I won *that* game. Of course."

"Only because I wasn't here," Kari teased. "I'm getting good, thanks to your tips. I may be even better than you, now."

"Not yet, Kari." Luke laughed. "Give yourself some time."

"Adventure can look like many different things." Dad took another serving of soup. "This afternoon, making dinner was a Monday adventure for me."

"Hey, you're right." Ashley sat a little straighter. "Every day of life can be an adventure. If you see it that way."

"That's right." Mom smiled at their father. "Any day and anywhere. You don't have to go far to have an adventure, either."

When dinner was over, they all helped with the dishes.

Kari studied her family getting things cleaned

up. This moment was like every other night. Some people might have said it was boring. But it wasn't at all. It was happy and silly and something Kari was only just now really seeing.

It was beautiful.

A few hours later, Kari hugged her parents good night.

Mom winked at her. "You smell like campfire."

"Best smell, right?" Kari could hear the joy in her own voice. Even the smoky bonfire last night had been a thrill.

Kari walked to the kitchen, grabbed her bags, and hurried up the stairs to her room.

Ashley was already there, working on a sketch. She looked up at Kari. "See? This is Clarence, flying low over the bus with friendly bears waving from the side of the road." Ashley squinted. "I didn't see them. But they were there. I know it."

Kari tossed the clothes from her bag in the dirty hamper and grabbed her journal from her backpack. What her dad had said at the dinner table still rang through her head. It was not only the perfect thought of the day. But it was the best final reminder for adventuring. She had to add it.

Kari flopped on her bed and read over her list. Yes, one more reminder and she would be ready for anything.

> Kari Baxter's Reminders for Enjoying Any Adventure
>
> Expect the unexpected.
> Try new things.
> Confidence is key.
> Always be prepared.

And finally, the last reminder:

> Adventures can happen anytime and anywhere.

She stared at the list. It finally felt complete. Also, it was a list made from experience, which was the best kind of list. Dad was right. Like always. Reminder number five was not just true about adventures. It was true about happy times in life.

She added one final thought:

Hi there, it's me. I'm so glad I allowed
adventures into my life these last few
days. It wasn't easy. But it's okay
because I learned and I grew, even on
the inside. And now I feel ready. I'll use
this list over and over again. And I'll be
fearless. That's all for now.

Kari shut her journal and as she did, she lay back and grinned at the ceiling. *Thank You, God. I couldn't have had fun these past few days without You.*

Kari didn't know what the next chapter held. But she was excited about all the adventures that awaited her and her amazing family. From here on out, Kari was determined to make every adventure, big or small, the absolute greatest it could be.

Because with a family like hers, each adventure was bound to be better than the last.

About the Authors

Karen Kingsbury, #1 *New York Times* bestselling novelist, is America's favorite inspirational storyteller, with more than twenty-five million of her award-winning books in print. Her last dozen titles have topped bestseller lists and many of her novels are under development as major motion pictures. Her Baxter Family books have been developed into a TV series slated to debut soon. Karen is also an adjunct professor of writing at Liberty University. She and her husband, Donald, live in Tennessee near their children and grandchildren.

Tyler Russell has been telling stories his whole life. In elementary school, he won a national award for a children's book he wrote. Since then, he hasn't stopped writing. In 2015, he graduated with a BFA from Lipscomb University. He sold his first screenplay, *Karen Kingsbury's Maggie's Christmas Miracle*, which premiered on Hallmark. Along with screenplays and novels, Tyler is a songwriter, singer, actor, and creative who lives in Nashville, Tennessee.